fatal love

ANATASI FAMILY SYNDICATE

BOOK 3

DORI PULITANO

Fatal Love
Copyright © 2024

Editor: Amy Briggs EditsByAmy.com
Cover Design: Taylored Designs

Author Dori Pulitano
www.AuthorDoriPulitano.com

This book has been re-edited to include new content.

family tree

Giuseppe Anastasi & Vittoria Anastasi
Grandfather/Deceased & Grandmother

Giacomo Anastasi
Godfather of Syndicate

Giorga Anastasi
Giacomo's Wife

Massimo Anastasi
28 years old
Don/Capo Famiglia
7-7-1996
Velvet Ace Lounge &
Casino

Madison Heart
20 years old
College Student
4-31-2004

Vincenzo Anastasi
26 years old
Underboss
5-18-1998
The Sapphire Dagger

Riley Rebecca Lawson
26 years old
Chef
1-16-1998
The Sapphire Dagger

Antonio Anastasi
24 years old
Captain/Caporegime
11-3-1999
Emerald Ace
Holdings

Mia Holly Hill
25 years old
Assistant DA
9-14-1998
Las Vegas District
Attorney

**Michael Daniel
Brighton**
26 years old
Attorney
6-4-1998
Anastasi Family Attorney

FAMILY TREE

Catarina Anastasi
26 years old
ER Nurse
8-9-1997

Celestina Anastasi
21 years old
College Student
10-1-2002

Carmela Anastasi
21 years old
College Student
10-1-2002

notable characters

Donny Cesare Russo
Consigliere/Capo

Drew Mancini
Enforcer

Kevin Luchasi
Anastasi Family Doctor

Manuel Costa
Javier's Brother

Cristian Silva
Chilean Mafia Underboss

Filippo Bianchi
Godfather Rome Italy Mafia

Sofia Bianchi
Underboss Reno Mafia

NOTABLE CHARACTERS

Carlisle Casteneli
Manager/Bartender Velvet Ace

Miguel Angel
Sureños Leader

Javier Costa
Sureños Former Leader

Matias Silva
Head of Chilean Mafia

Bastian Silva
Chilean Mafia Captain/Caporegime

Lorenzo Bianchi
Don Reno Mafia

series reading order

DANGEROUS ATTRACTION

MASSIMO & MADISON'S BOOK

DARK DESIRE

VINCENZO & RILEY'S BOOK

FATAL LOVE

ANTONIO, RACHEL & MICHAEL'S BOOK

DEADLY INTENTIONS

CATARINA & DONNY'S BOOK

CARNAGE HEART (NOVELLA)

BECKETT'S STORY

SAVAGE HEARTS

CELESTINA & BECKETT'S STORY

UNFORESEEN LOYALTY

A SHORT STORY

FRACTURED DEVOTION

CARMELLA & ALEX'S BOOK

Grab the entire series on E-Book at
https://alphabookboyfriends.com/collections/bundles/bundles

reader warning

Like most Mafia books, this series contains scenes that may be difficult for some to handle. Human trafficking, violence, male/male/female romance, kidnapping, and attempted suicide are addressed throughout the six-book series.

If that is not something you can handle, please discontinue reading.

Suicide is a serious matter. If you or anyone you know in the United States is contemplating suicide, please seek help by reaching out to Lifeline at https://988lifeline.org/ or by dialing 988 from your phone. International assistance is available by visiting https://blog.opencounseling.com/suicide-hotlines/

More than 27 million people around the world endure the abhorrent abuse of human trafficking and forced labor, including thousands of people right here in the United States. It is a threat to global security, public safety, and human dignity. If you believe you are a victim of human trafficking or may have information about a potential trafficking situation, don't hesitate to get in touch with the U.S. National Human Trafficking Hotline at https://humantraffickinghotline.org/. If you or someone you know is in immediate danger, please call 911.

When it comes to finding love… don't be the only
thing standing in your way.

UNKNOWN

one

ANTONIO

STANDING outside Mia Hill's house, my mind was a whirlpool of thoughts and emotions. I glanced around the quiet suburban neighborhood, the neatly trimmed lawns and peaceful atmosphere a stark contrast to the turmoil brewing inside me. My heart pounded with the weight of my mission and the recent confrontation with Michael. But now wasn't the time to dwell on personal matters. I had a job to do, and Riley's future depended on it.

Diego, one of the guys Miguel had planted inside Mia's house through a subsidy of Emerald Ace Holdings, the business I ran for the family, stood next to me. We blended into the shadows cast by the tall hedges. Diego was reliable, resourceful, and most importantly, discreet. I trusted Miguel Angel when he had recommended him for the job. And tonight, I was counting on Diego's expertise to get the job done.

"Is everything ready?" I asked, my voice low and steady, masking the anxiety bubbling beneath the surface.

Diego nodded, his eyes sharp and focused. "Yes, everything's set. We just need to replace her current cameras with ours and then add a few in places she won't see them. I've already disarmed her current alarm."

I took a deep breath and nodded in agreement. "Good. We can't afford to make any mistakes. Riley's trial is coming up fast, and we need something substantial to turn the tide in our favor."

Diego's gaze flicked to mine, a hint of concern in his eyes. "You sure about this, sir? I mean, planting cameras in her house… it's risky. If we get caught—" He took a breath. "It's risky enough being here as her contractor."

"We won't get caught," I interjected, my tone firm. "We can't afford to think like that. We need leverage, and this is the best way to get it. Mia has a kinky past, and if we can catch her in something recent, then ruining her credibility could be the break we need. "

Diego nodded, his resolve hardening. "All right."

I glanced at my watch. "She should be home in an hour, that doesn't give us much time, but I trust we can get it done. Remember, we need the cameras in the main living areas, her office, and her bedroom. Focus on places where she might engage in any… compromising activities. Michael assured me one small fracture in her professional allure is all it would take to make the department pull her from this high-profile case."

My mind wandered back to the conversation with Michael. The hurt and confusion in Michael's eyes had haunted me since that night. I knew I had acted out of fear, pushing Michael away to protect myself. But now, standing on the brink of something that could cost me everything, I couldn't help but think about the consequences of my actions.

We approached the house with practiced stealth, slipping through the side gate and making our way to a side door that Diego had previously unlocked. Inside, the house was dimly lit, the faint hum of appliances the only sound.

Diego pulled out a small case from his backpack, filled with the tiny, high-tech cameras they would be planting. He handed a few to me, and we immediately split up to cover more ground.

I moved silently through the house, my senses heightened by the adrenaline coursing through my veins. I placed the first camera in the living room, hiding it carefully among the decorative items on a shelf. The second camera went in the kitchen, positioned to cover the most commonly used areas.

As I moved to the stairs, I heard Diego working quietly in the office, his movements efficient and precise. I made my way to the bedroom, the most crucial location. I placed a camera near the bed, ensuring it had a clear view of the room. A part of me couldn't help but feel a pang of guilt invading some-one's private space like this, but I reminded him of the stakes.

With the cameras in place, Diego and I regrouped in the hallway.

"All set?" I whispered.

Diego nodded. "All set. We should get out of here before she comes back."

We retraced their steps, slipping out of the house and back into the safety of the shadows outside. As we moved away from the house, I felt a mixture of relief and tension. The cameras were in place, but now came the waiting game. My family needed Mia to provide us with the ammunition we could use to discredit her and turn the trial in Riley's favor.

"Good work, Diego," I said quietly as we reached the end of the street. "Now we wait."

Diego gave a tight smile. "You got it, boss. We'll get what we need."

I nodded, watching as Diego disappeared into the night. Alone with my thoughts, I couldn't shake the feeling of unease that lingered. The mission had gone smoothly, but the stakes were higher than ever. Riley's future, my family's reputation, and now, the unresolved tension with Michael all weighed heavily on my mind.

As I made my way back to my car, I took a deep breath, steeling myself for the challenges ahead. I couldn't afford to let my personal turmoil distract me. I had to stay focused and determined to do whatever it took to protect my family and ensure Riley's freedom.

two

MIA

EVEN WITH THE phone held out from my face, I could hear the frustration in the district attorney, Mike Donovan's voice, "What do you mean you don't have anything? If we're going to put a former FBI agent in jail—a pregnant one at that—you better have evidence proving she planned to kill him. If you can't make this stick, Mia, your career will be over. Do you understand what I am saying to you? Get a fucking extension and find what we need to get that guilty verdict… and soon."

"Yeah. I hear you." I slammed the phone down, pissed off. It was getting old listening to Donovan's demands. My team of investigators hadn't found a damn thing that proved Riley Lawson—now Anastasi—maliciously sought to kill a man. A man who, for all accounts, deserved death.

Donat Ivanov might not have been as evil as his brother, Dmitri, but he hadn't been a good guy. Not to mention the fact he showed up at Vincenzo Anastasi's restaurant unannounced—you can bet it wasn't for tea and cookies.

They were fucking this case up hand over foot, and I didn't think I'd get it back under control. Hell, I didn't even think Riley was guilty of manslaughter. I learned shortly after arriving in this city the feds were going after her because they wanted her husband. It certainly wasn't because there was no hard proof of her guilt. The only thing that woman was guilty of was falling in love with a mobster. And now, she was pregnant with Vincenzo Anastasi's baby. If I was going to find some sort of motive, I needed to delay the trial and try to get shit back under control. I hated delaying cases, but if I didn't, we had no chance of winning.

"Judge Crowder's office," the soft voice of his secretary filtered through the phone.

"Jessica, this is Mia Hill." I put on my fake sweetness as I spoke. Sweet was not how people back home would describe me. Bitch, ice queen, cunt, maybe…but not sweet. "Is Judge Crawford available?"

"Ms. Hill, he just hung up from another call. Hang on, and I'll patch you through. We should get drinks sometime."

"That sounds good. Call me this weekend." With bated breath, I waited for him to answer. He was a fair man, so hopefully, he'd see reason and grant me the request.

"This better be good. I was about to head home."

"Your Honor, I'm sorry to postpone your departure, but I need a favor." I paused and took a breath. "I need a delay for the Lawson, rather, Anastasi trial." I corrected myself.

"Fuck, Hill. You realize delaying gives the opposing side more ammo against the prosecution, right?"

"Yes, Sir, but we don't have enough evidence to show she *wanted* to kill him. I'm beginning to believe it was mere happenstance that she was the one there and not Vincenzo Anastasi."

His sigh filled the line. "If you don't think *Mrs*. Anastasi did it, it's your job… no, it's your oath to dismiss this case. I know the FBI has a hard-on for the Anastasi family. Still, if this is really a case of mistaken identity… and as you call it, *happenstance,*"—his heavy sigh vibrated the speaker against my ear— "then putting a pregnant woman behind bars would be wrong and career suicide."

"My thoughts exactly."

"Fine, I'll delay it for a couple of weeks. Make sure you notify the opposing counsel. I'm certain they aren't going to be sad it's being postponed."

"Thank you, Judge."

I held the receiver in my hand and closed my eyes. For my entire life, I had pressured myself to be the toughest prosecutor around, but lately, I felt like it wasn't enough. This case weighed heavily on me. Riley had been one of the best at her job, too. Hell, she'd been recruited by the FBI at a young age. But falling in love had changed her, making her priorities shift so much, she'd risked not only her career but her freedom.

Would love change my outlook on things?

I shook the thought out of my head and clicked around on my computer until I found Riley Anastasi's attorney information.

Michael Brighton.

He was new on the Anastasi family's team of lawyers, but his reputation proved strong. I met him once…before I knew who he was. The moment I learned he was Riley's attorney, I steered clear. But damn, he was good-looking and had tempted me in ways that almost made me throw caution to the wind. I hated the way his captivating stare made me feel that night—it still haunted my dreams.

Dialing his number, I pressed the phone to my ear and waited.

"Michael Brighton," his deep voice filled the line, making me flush with heat.

Every time I heard from him, my body reacted the same way. I was dreading having to be in the same room as him for court. If my body responded to just the sound of his voice, there was no telling how it would react to being in his presence.

I took a deep breath, willing the pounding in my chest to stop. He was the opposing counsel, and feeling this way about him was wrong on so many levels.

"Hello?"

"Shit…" I murmured into the phone. "I'm sorry… Mr. Brighton, this is Mia Hill. I'm calling about your client, Riley Anastasi."

His chuckle told me he'd heard my slip of the tongue. "Are you calling to dismiss the ridiculous case you have against her?" His tone was mocking, but beneath that, it was laced with something else—something I needed to ignore.

"What? No. I'm calling to let you know the trial has been delayed. I'll send you the paperwork tomorrow."

His growl should have irritated me, but as usual, it didn't. "I want to see the paperwork tonight. Bring it to my office since I'm here working late on *this* case."

"Are you serious? I can have a courier bring it to you in the morning."

"On Saturday?" Another chuckle had me rolling my eyes. "I doubt that will happen, and I'm not waiting until Monday."

Fuck, I'd forgotten it was Friday. Most people would be out and about, but not me. I had no life outside of this job. "Fine," I relented, knowing he'd make this more of an issue than I needed to risk. "I'll bring it by on my way home. Will you still be there in an hour?"

"Well… as I just said, I'm working late because of a bogus case against a client. A case that requires overtime to clear her name."

"Funny, Mr. Brighton." I rolled my eyes at his poor attempt to be funny. "I didn't realize you were a comedian as well. Anyway, I'll see you in about an hour."

After disconnecting the call, I turned back to my computer. I needed to find something proving guilt, and I needed it fast. An hour later, still coming up empty-handed, I slammed my laptop closed and tossed it into my bag. Shoving the file, along with the printed order from the judge that'd been delivered by courier thirty minutes earlier, I headed out.

My stomach growled, reminding me I hadn't eaten since breakfast. After an internal debate, I decided to bring food to Michael as an apology for the inconvenience of waiting for me. The truth was, with Riley pregnant, I knew they wanted this wrapped up soon, and a delay would put her closer to her due date. Deep down, I wanted to find the evidence that either cleared her name or allowed me to put her behind bars—the waiting was killing us all.

The law office where Michael worked was a modern building. It differed entirely from the county offices I worked out of—mainly because it was new and not decrepit like the thirty-year-old building the city used. I threw my bag over my shoulder and cradled the bag of food in my elbow as I headed toward the door. It was locked, forcing me to knock. My knuckles tapped across the glass pane, echoing through the empty space. For whatever reason, I was nervous. This was the second time I'd see him face to face—the first time was something I had pushed far from my memory, or at least tried to.

My gaze followed the silhouette of a man walking toward the door. Even from a distance and in the darkened room, I could tell he was tall and built. As he got closer, my stomach coiled with a familiar flutter. The man staring at me from the other side of the glass tied my insides in knots just by being... *alive*. This was going to test my restraint. There was no denying I wanted him. I had wanted him all those nights ago but walked away. Staring at him now, I wasn't sure I'd be able to do it a second time if given the opportunity to decide.

"Miss. Hill?" He opened the door and ushered me inside.

His formality made me think the attraction may be one-sided, which would make remaining professional easy.

"I think you can call me Mia unless we're in court, seeing as we're already acquainted." I shot him a wicked grin, expecting him to be stone-faced.

He wasn't.

"Of course, Mia." His eyes smoldered as he sucked on his bottom lip. "You have the order?"

I couldn't tear my gaze off his lips. His chuckle snapped me out of it, and I turned toward what I assumed was his office.

"Oh, yeah, and dinner. I thought…" What was I thinking by bringing dinner to the enemy's office? He was the enemy, right?

The sound of his footsteps told me he followed me. "You brought dinner, too?"

"I inconvenienced you by making you stay late." I set the food down on the desktop. "This is my way of apologizing. I know we are on opposite sides, but we both want the same thing… the truth."

"And what is the truth? My client acted in self-defense, yet your department wants to throw her in jail. I know they have a hard-on for the Anastasi family, but this is crossing a line."

I turned my body and stared at him.

He was right in the fact that they were using Riley to break the family—or, specifically, Vincenzo Anastasi, who was in love with her. This was their way of getting him to crack or slip up.

"You're right, but that's why I asked for more time. Either I'll find evidence proving the charges or proving her innocence." I turned back toward his desk and started pulling the containers out.

Michael stepped closer, and I could feel his body's heat as he pressed in behind me.

"Let me help you." His breath brushed against my neck.

Reaching around me, he set down some plates, and his arm brushed against mine. Tiny electric tendrils danced across my skin, making me suck in a breath. Every nerve was firing on overdrive, making my head spin in confusion.

"Sorry," I whispered. "I should go… this was a mistake." I slipped beneath his arm and started toward the door.

"Mia, wait." His long legs had him standing in front of me in two strides. "Tell me you feel it." Michael stepped forward and cupped my face.

"Feel what?" My eyes closed as his thumb brushed across my bottom lip.

"I know this is probably fucked up, but I want you. The moment you walked into my office, I was hit with the same need to possess you as before." His hand tilted my head up. "The tension… the pull." He licked his lips, his eyes darkening as he moved closer. "You still feel it, too, don't you?"

"Yes," I whispered, my gaze never leaving his. "But I'm the prosecutor on your client's case. It's a bad idea."

He drew his bottom lip into his mouth, a battle waging in his head.

"Fuck *it*."

Michael's head descended, his lips pressing against mine as he took what he wanted—what we both wanted. I whimpered as my body melted into his hold. The kiss consumed me like flames burning through a forest, leaving nothing but ash behind. His free hand tugged my hip, pulling me even closer as his tongue slipped between the seam of my mouth. His kiss demanded ownership, taking control of every rational thought. Michael's growl, coupled with the ever-growing bulge pressing against my belly, had me pulsing with desire. He was turning me on like no one ever had before.

The vibration of my phone inside my pocket was like a bucket of cold water, jerking me from the disaster in waiting. I took a step back. A look of confusion marred his features— the same one I was sure was painted across my face.

Pulling the cockblocker from my pocket, I pressed it to my face.

"Hello?" My gaze never wavered from Michael's as I listened to the voice on the other end. I was still caught between heaven and hell, not really registering their words before I hung up. "I have to go."

Turning without a word, I hurried through the office and out the glass door. Michael was still staring at me from behind the glass when I finally glanced back. What happened was wrong—but God, it felt so right. His expression was one of hurt and confusion, but what I didn't see was regret, and that left me lost.

Slipping into my car, I slammed the door and pressed my head to the steering wheel. These muddled feelings between us could ruin me as an attorney—and destroy any case against Riley.

I stopped my car before pulling it onto the road and glanced in my rearview mirror. I'm not sure why I did, but my breath hitched when I found Michael still watching me. Even from my car, his piercing green eyes bore into me, begging me to turn around. I glanced away and pulled out of the parking lot —away from the man who could ultimately destroy me. As much as I wanted him, it couldn't happen.

Not *now*.

Maybe *never*.

three

ANOTNIO

FUCK.

I stared down at the water bubbling up from the wooden floorboards. A pipe had burst, creating the monsoon of water pouring out. Diego called panicked since this was outside his wheelhouse of expertise and called me when the catastrophe happened. As soon as I got here, I began tearing up the floor after sending Diego to the hardware store for some supplies. I glanced at my watch, praying Mia wouldn't get home anytime soon.

The last thing I needed was her catching me here—if she did, my entire plan would be fucked. Having unfiltered access to her house had given me a bird's eye view to her outside of her working career. From what I'd learned, Mia lived a normal life—except for the dirty past Michael dug up a few months ago.

Michael.

Even thinking about him made my chest tighten. His words

rang in my ears like thunder on repeat— *When you're ready to admit how you feel, call me.*

I wanted to tell him he was right, that I wanted him more than my next breath, but how could I do that when I couldn't even admit it to myself *or* to my family? I closed my eyes as I drove the wedge into the floor. My grandfather had known the real me and accepted it without hesitation. He argued that I was wrong about how the family would react, but I couldn't bear their rejection if he was wrong.

The only other person I'd confided in was Madison—my brother, Massimo's fiancée. I was thrilled when Madison came into his life, but even more grateful to have her in mine. She got me on levels no one else did, a lot like my grandfather had. They were alike in the sense she wanted me to be honest with everyone and let them in, but fear paralyzed me like prey caught in a predator's sights.

"Um? What the fuck are you doing here?" The tapping of a shoe and the slurred words jerked me from my thoughts.

The hammer slipped from my hand, slamming down on the hand palm flattened against the plank of wood. "Shit." Glancing up, my eyes connected with none other than Mia Hill.

Despite the venomous glare, Mia Hill was sex on a stick. Her narrowed eyes and the way she folded her arms across her chest only made her sexier. Her hair was pulled back into a sleek ponytail, showing off the perfect apple shape of her face and her sexy as fuck neck—a neck that led down to perfect curves.

"You had a pipe burst," I explained, swallowing the nerves this woman created. "I'm trying to tear up the floor to seal it off. Otherwise, you're going to be swimming tonight." I turned and continued working. The grunt of disapproval made me look back at her. "What?"

Her eyes blinked as she pursed her lips. "How the hell did you get into my house? I've never seen you here. In fact," She tossed her purse on the counter. "Where's Diego. I'm calling him."

"I'm on the crew doing your remodel. And Diego went to buy something to fix this mess. He'll be back in a few..."

"What the fuck are you talking about?" She closed her eyes and wavered on her feet, clearly drunk. "And why is there water everywhere?"

She threw her hands up in the air and stormed past me. Mia wasn't paying attention and as soon as her heel hit the slick hardwoods not ripped up, her body slipped, throwing her off balance. I dropped the hammer again and lunged forward, catching her in my arms.

"Um." Diego cleared his throat. "I got the materials we need." He was staring at me with a look of fear. I mean, fuck, I was holding the woman who had the power to destroy my entire family.

"It's fine, Diego. You can go—I'll take care of this."

He furrowed his brows in confusion. "You sure that's a good idea?"

It was probably not a good idea, but I nodded anyway. "Yeah. I'm going to just help her out and we'll tackle this mess in the morning."

Diego gave me one last look, then turned and stormed out of the room. I glanced down at the woman still clutching to my shirt, "You okay?"

Her eyes were wide in shock. "No. I'm not." She blinked, her eyes crinkling with laughter that erupted as if she was a deranged person. "I just about made out with…" She jerked her body from my grasp and pushed herself to her feet. "It doesn't matter. I've had a bit too much to drink and probably shouldn't have driven myself home. But I did. And guess what? *I don't give a fuck.* I think the gods are trying to tell me something." She stared at me a moment. "You're really hot."

After the shock of her words wore off, I realized she didn't recognize me—an obvious side effect of the alcohol seeping out of her pores.

"Wait. You drove home drunk?" Looking at her more closely, I realized she was nearly three sheets to the wind and could barely stand. I didn't know how the hell she made it home without killing herself. She could barely make out the dangers in the kitchen—and I didn't just mean the wet floor.

"Yep." She cocked an eyebrow. "You gonna call the cops? No." Mia braced her hand on the counter and pointed at me. "Don't answer that. I don't care. I am so over this fucking town."

I watched in shock as she pulled a bottle of whiskey from the cabinet, uncapped it, and pressed it to her lips. My cock hardened as I watched her suck down the amber liquid without so much as a flinch.

"When they asked me to come down here from New York, I didn't know I was going to be plopped right into the middle of some pissing contest. They hate the Anastasi family so much, they're willing to lie about someone's guilt to bring them down."

"Who hates who?" I knew exactly what she said but wanted to see what else she'd say. The alcohol was making her super lax about what she was sharing, something I knew she wouldn't do had she been sober. But this was the opening I needed to get her to slip up and say something that could help Riley's case.

"The FBI, the DA's office, hell, everyone that isn't on their payroll. They have a fucking hard-on for them and want to make an example out of…oh, never mind." She waved her hand through the air before grabbing the bottle again. My eyes were riveted to her mouth as she wrapped her lips around the bottle and took another pull of its contents.

"The thing is… I don't think the suspect is guilty. At least not how their trying to make her. Tonight, when I asked for an extension on the trial, it was because I don't have enough evidence to put her away."

I leaned against the kitchen table, listening as she kept rambling on. Somehow, she'd become the leaky pipe, and I wanted to caulk her—but not to stop the noise coming out of her mouth.

"I left New York because I felt empty. I was a badass there. Did you know that?"

"Can't say that I did." I shifted uncomfortably, trying to casually adjust my hard-on so she couldn't see.

"My boss basically told me if I don't put her behind bars, my career is done. And you know what?" She drank again, the bottle half empty now. She had downed half a bottle of whiskey in under fifteen minutes. "I don't *fucking* care." She slung the bottle around dramatically, splashing some of the liquor on her hand. "I want a life. I want to feel loved. Do you know how long it's been since I've had sex?" Her expression became serious as she turned her gaze to me. "Months… Pathetic, right?"

Stepping forward, I grabbed the whiskey from her and dropped it into the sink. "Hey, I think you should go lay down. You've clearly had a long day, and I don't want you to say something you'll regret in the morning when you remember this moment."

Mia pressed her palms to her head and groaned. "The only thing I regret is not fucking the hot man I just left."

"All right, gorgeous." I wrapped my fingers around her arm. "Let me help you to your bed, then I'll finish here and lock up." Something about seeing her so vulnerable had me regretting my motives for being in her house. "Let's get you to your bed… you need to sleep this off." It was clear she was torn about the case, but pressure from the district attorney and the FBI had her scrambling to put Riley away.

"My life is so fucked up." She shook her head and turned toward me. "You think I'm gorgeous?" She pressed her palm against my chest, the smell of whiskey on her breath. "You're fucking *hot*."

The T-shirt I was wearing was still wet from the broken pipe, making it stick to me like a second skin. Her fingernails scraped across the front of my shirt, spurring the already hardening of my dick into overdrive. I'd seen photos of her that made my mind picture her in ways I shouldn't but having her this close and personal was like a real life fantasy come true.

"Thanks…" I mumbled, navigating the two of us up the stairs.

She jerked to a stop and leaned back. Her eyes narrowed as if she was trying to focus them better. "I don't even know your name. How is it I don't know you?"

"My name isn't important right now. Getting you into bed is." Relieved that her drunkenness was protecting my identity, I wasn't about to give her my name.

"I want to forget about everything." She sighed and half-walked, half-stumbled toward her bedroom door. Pausing with her hand braced against the wall, she turned to look back at me. "Can you help me?"

Assuming she meant help with the door, I moved around her and fisted the doorknob. "Here you—" The sudden impact of her body against mine cut off what I was going to say. Mia rubbed her breasts against me as her fingers fisted the clingy material covering my skin. "Whoa… Mia. What are you doing?" I could feel the heat of her core against my thigh, despite the material separating us.

"I need something good to happen…and this—" Her hand slid down my front and cupped my crotch. "Feels like it would be pretty good."

My eyes drifted shut at the glorious sensation of her fingers squeezing me. "God… Mia—" I growled her name, taking slow measured breaths I grabbed her hand and stilled her movement. "Look… as much as I'd enjoy this, you don't know me, and you're drunk." My dick, against my silent plea to stand down, was threatening to bust my zipper.

"I don't think he got the memo." She licked her lips and squeezed again. "I'm drunk and asking you... no telling you to *fuck* me. I'm sure a guy like you has had a one-night stand before. So, man up and do me a solid... let me see that cock."

She pinched the zipper between her fingers and slowly lowered the metal barrier. I froze, my body begging me to stay... my brain screaming for me to run. When her fingers brushed against the smooth skin of my shaft, my jaw clenched.

"I *should* go."

All rational thoughts flew out the window when her fingers wrapped around my cock, and she pulled me free. "You sure?" Mia's hand moved along the exposed length. The soft giggle she emitted reminded me she was not in her right mind, causing me to step back.

"You're not in your right mind. I think you should sleep this off. When you sober up, you'll probably regret this whole conversation."

Her hold on my shaft tightened instead of letting it go. Mia pushed me against the wall and dropped to her knees. "I'm not that drunk."

The air whooshed out of my lungs as her warm mouth wrapped around my cockhead. It was unlike anything I could have imagined. When her head bobbed, coupled with the perfect amount of suction, I nearly passed out from the sensation.

I bucked against her as my hand wound the ponytail around my wrist, so I could hold her in place as she worked me like a magician. The sound of her lips smacking against my dick made me harden more—something I didn't think was possible. I jerked her head back, pulling her off my crown, not wanting to finish in her throat.

"I don't want to come in your mouth." No longer caring whether this was the right thing to do, I lifted her feet off the floor and carried her toward the bed. Our mouths met in a frenzy as we toppled to the mattress. "You're sure you want this, Mia?"

"Yes." Her fingers tugged at the cotton fabric, urging me to strip it off. "Clothes off *now*."

Standing, I shed my shirt and pants like a chameleon sheds his skin. Mia wiggled out of her work clothes, revealing a sexy lace bra and matching thong.

"Fuck, gorgeous, if I'd known you had this hiding under your clothes, I would have buried myself inside you earlier." The electric energy filled the room as I reached down and brushed my palm across the see-through material. "As nice as these are, I need them gone." The material ripped with ease as I tore them from her center. "Please tell me you have a condom."

Mia rolled over and jerked open the drawer. Leaning up on her knees, she ripped the foil packet with her teeth and beckoned me forward with the crook of her finger. My dick twitched beneath her touch as she rolled the barrier over my shaft with precision. I didn't want to think about why this woman was so good at covering a man in a rubber. The possessive feeling associated with it was not something I wanted to deal with—especially not when she laid on her back and spread her legs.

Seeing her glistening pink pussy made me want to take my time with her—but that's not what this was. This was just sex. At least that's the mantra I kept telling myself as I buried myself inside her. Our bodies rocked in a rhythm that was almost perfect as we raced toward our release.

When her walls tightened around me in a vise grip, I shattered right along with her. The force threatened to burst the condom as I spilled myself inside her, my body jerking with uncontrollable movements. I'd never experienced a release quite so explosive. When our breathing finally slowed, I pressed my lips to hers, the sound of my heart drumming wildly against my ribs as I claimed her mouth again. Overwhelmed with the bizarre feelings this woman was creating inside me, I pulled out and retreated to the bathroom.

Stripping the used condom off my flaccid dick, I tossed it into the wastebasket and decided it was time to go. When I stepped back into the bedroom, I smiled at the sexy sight of her passed out and curled into a ball on the bed. I tugged the covers over her sleeping frame, then kissed her shoulder. Pulling on my pants, I fisted the wet shirt in my hand and started out the door. Glancing at her one last time, I forced myself to pull the bedroom door closed and walk away.

If I was lucky, Mia wouldn't remember this tomorrow—although the alpha in me wanted her to. She'd shared a lot of things with me... things that could destroy her case. *Things* I should share with Michael and my brothers.

The question was—did I want to tell them so we could use it against her?

My mind wandered back to Michael, and a pang of guilt riddled my system. To Mia, what we'd just shared was just sex. But even thinking about her body wrapped around mine, I couldn't deny I wished it could've been something more.

I hurried through the house, ensuring it was locked up tight. My heart tightened in my chest as I made my way to my car. I was quite sure I was fucked, no matter what I did.

Not even sure why I was doing it, I found myself driving toward Michael's house. Even after I'd fucked Mia, Michael was at the forefront of my thoughts.

God, I was fucked up.

MIA

MY HEAD THUMPED like a train rushing down the tracks, threatening to derail as I peeled open my eyes. Pain stabbed through my temples, a cruel reminder of the gallons of liquor I downed and the reckless decision to drive home drunk. Memories of the night before were foggy at best, but one vivid recollection burned into my mind: the delicious ache between my legs. Without that soreness, I might have dismissed the incredible sex as a vivid dream. I'd thrown myself at the hammer-wielding contractor who had been on his knees in my kitchen. He rejected me at first, but the moment my mouth wrapped around his cock, his resolve crumbled. And damn. When he tossed me onto the bed... it was the best sex I'd ever had. My core pulsed at the memory, making me squeeze my thighs together in a futile attempt to dampen the rising heat.

Staring at the ceiling, self-loathing seeped in as I recalled why I'd gotten so drunk in the first place. My boss had all but threatened my position, and in a moment of sheer madness, I'd kissed the opposing attorney.

"*Fuck.*" I groaned into the emptiness of the room, forcing myself to get out of bed despite the pounding in my head.

Michael Brighton was sexy, and I couldn't deny the magnetic pull I felt toward him, but my employer wouldn't care about his looks. If my boss ever found out I'd kissed him, crossing a serious boundary, I'd be fired on the spot.

So, what did I do? I went and fucked a stranger. Flashes of his muscular body infiltrated my mind—particularly the image of him looking down at me while I pleasured him. He seemed so familiar, and I cursed myself for not getting his name, but at that moment, his impressive length was all that mattered.

Thinking about him was the last thing I should be doing, but the memories of how he commanded my body, effortlessly triggering my orgasm, made my skin flush with heat. I clenched my phone, wavering on whether to call my contractor to get his name and number. Just as I summoned the nerve, my phone vibrated, derailing my plan.

Glancing at the screen, I grimaced when I saw it was the very person who could destroy me with a single stroke of his pen —my boss. If he was calling me on a Saturday, it couldn't be good. Praying my voice didn't betray the hangover I was battling, I pressed talk.

"This is Mia."

As suspected, his pissed-off tone blurted through the speaker.

"Miss Hill."

"Yes, Sir?" The formality of him using my surname raised my hackles, a surge of defensiveness washing over me.

"Why were you seen coming out of the opposing attorney's office last night?"

"I'm sorry, what did you say?" I pinched the bridge of my nose in frustration, the pressure doing little to alleviate the pounding headache.

"You were seen leaving Mr. Brighton's office late last night. Care to explain why?"

What in the hell? My anger flared, caught between indignation at being tattled on and the absurdity of him demanding an explanation.

"Well, sir, I dropped off the order from the judge. Remember? The one you suggested I get to delay the trial. He wanted a copy, and he wanted it in hand. What the hell? Since when is it a crime to go to the other attorney's office?"

He mumbled something under his breath before sighing heavily. "Nothing else happened?"

I thought back to the taste of Michael's lips on mine and swallowed hard, the lie burning my throat. "No. Nothing." My anger dissipated slightly, replaced by a gnawing sense of unease. I took a breath, steadying my voice. "What's going on, Mike?"

"It would appear you're being followed by someone, and whoever it is wants to bring this case down by any means they can. You need to be careful until we go to trial. Do you understand me? We don't need any missteps."

"Understood." Crap on a cracker. This wasn't something I needed right now. "But I'd like to know who's following me."

"Me, too. Just be careful until I can sort it out."

I disconnected the call, feeling a red-hot rage simmer beneath my skin. The betrayal stung, a mixture of fear and anger churning in my gut.

Had Michael sold me out? The question gnawed at me, twisting my insides. I couldn't shake the image of his familiar eyes, the way they had darkened with desire. Was it all a facade? Was he playing a deeper game? My mind whirled with possibilities, each one darker than the last.

I needed answers, but more than that, I needed to protect myself. The stakes had just gotten higher, and trust was a luxury I couldn't afford.

There was only one way to find out, and I planned to ask the man in question in person. I wasn't going to give him any opportunity to avoid me or lie to me. I plugged my phone up to charge while I showered, the hot water scalding my skin but failing to soothe the seething anger within. If Michael Brighton had any role in this stupid stunt, I'd destroy him. As soon as I got upstairs, I grabbed my laptop and flicked it open, fingers flying over the keys as I searched for his contact information. If he or his client weren't having me followed, then we'd have a whole new set of problems.

After finding his phone number, I dialed it with trembling fingers, a mixture of fury and fear fueling my determination. The ringing seemed to stretch on forever, each second amplifying my rage.

"This is Michael."

His voice caught me off guard, making me blank out for a

second. It was too smooth, too calm, for the storm brewing inside me.

"Are you having me followed?" There was no way he didn't detect my bitter tone. I was too pissed to stifle the rage or remain professional.

"What?" I could hear the sleepy sound in his voice, telling me I'd woken him up. "Mia?"

"Yes. Who the hell else would call you on a Saturday morning to ask such a ridiculous question?" I bit back, my teeth clenching with barely contained fury. "Well? Are you?"

"Give me a second. It's…" He paused, and I could hear the bed creak in the background. Someone else's hushed voice had me straining to hear. "It's seven in the morning. Can you start over? And maybe not rip my head off when you do."

I gritted my teeth, hissing out my reply. "Someone is following me. I want to know if it's you."

"Following you?" He repeated like he was having trouble following the conversation.

"Jesus Christ." I leaned my head back and blew out a frustrated breath. "Are you listening to me? Yes. Followed. My boss called me this morning, concerned I was compromising the case. Apparently, I was seen at your office last night, and they found it suspicious enough to call him. So, I'll ask again. Are you having me followed?"

"No." He laughed, a sound that grated on my nerves. "Why would I?"

"I don't know." I wanted to reach through the phone and

strangle him. "Maybe to create a scandal, so the case would be thrown out."

"The case will be dismissed whether I have you followed or not. Riley is innocent, and you know that. Now…" I could hear him breathe out, a heavy sigh. "The real question is, who is tipping off your superiors with such bogus complaints?"

"Maybe the Anastasi family is doing it and didn't tell you."

"Hang on." The rustling of the phone being covered echoed through the line. I could hear him talking and after a moment, he came back on the line. "No, it's not them."

"How the hell would you know that? Who are you talking to?" I pulled the device from my face and glanced at the screen, as if it would reveal the other person to me.

"That's not important, but you being followed concerns me."

My phone dinged with a text. When I pulled it away again, I saw the message was from Michael. "Why are you texting me when we're on the phone?"

"It's an address. Meet me there in two hours, so we can talk without the worry of being watched or listened in on."

"Shit. You think my phone is bugged, too? What's going on, Michael?"

There was nothing but silence for a beat of thirty seconds, the weight of it pressing down on me, then finally, his gruff voice came through the speaker. "Two hours, Mia."

The line went dead, leaving me a mass of confusion. I tried to search my brain for any possibilities of who would be following me but came up short. Since arriving in Vegas, I hadn't handled any major cases that would put me in the crosshairs of someone seeking vengeance. That left me with only one thought—it had to be related to this case.

After showering at the speed of light, I pulled my golden strands into a tight ponytail, not bothering with the time to dry it. I slipped into a pair of leggings and a T-shirt—my go-to Saturday attire. During the week, I always dressed professionally—heels, skirts, the typical attorney look—but today, I didn't give a rat's ass what anyone thought. Tying my shoes, I snagged my laptop and shoved it into my bag.

Once I was downstairs, I made myself some coffee, praying like hell it would alleviate the headache throbbing behind my eyes. I needed something to staunch the pain, so I could be on my game if I was going to risk seeing Michael. If someone was following me, getting to the address he sent was going to be tricky.

Sitting down, coffee in hand, I sifted through the documents I'd brought home. Riley was accused of manslaughter, and the feds were trying to make an example out of her. However, I knew they were really hoping to anger Vincenzo into admitting he was the one who'd killed Donat Ivanov. After all, it made more sense that he'd stabbed the man, not Riley, since everyone believed him to be the notorious La Lama. The odd thing was the evidence I had pointed to Dmitri Ivanov as being the Prizrak and La Lama, or that Dmitri at least controlled La Lama. There was no way La Lama was Vincenzo—the bad blood between Dmitri and him proved that.

Maybe Michael could shed some light on the questions I had. Deep down, my gut insisted Riley hadn't killed him intentionally or at all, but if it was her that wielded the knife, it was self-defense, plain and simple. Did they want Vincenzo so badly, they were willing to destroy one of their own? After staring at the useless information, I shoved it into my backpack and headed out.

Meeting Michael was a risk in more ways than one, but I was willing to take it if it meant getting answers. I stood for justice and truth—no matter which side that fell on.

ANTONIO

"I SHOULD GO." I stood and grabbed my shirt, shoving my arms into the sleeves. The guilt of the night's events weighed heavily on me. "I don't think I should be here when Mia arrives."

Michael walked up behind me and pressed his lips to my shoulder, a gesture that sent shivers down my spine. "Stop running, Antonio. You came here last night for a reason. And just like I told you then, I don't care that you slept with her. Hell, I wanted to bend her over my desk when she was in my office. She's fucking gorgeous."

"Right. Thanks for reminding me I was her second choice." I couldn't hide the bitterness in my voice. "You're the reason she was wasted when she got home. She drove like that. Did I tell you?"

"Yeah," Michael made a soft growling noise in his throat, a sound that usually thrilled me, but now just added to my frustration. "And we'll talk to her about being stupid when she gets here. For now, we need to figure out who is watching her because if they're watching her, you bet your ass they're watching Vincenzo and Riley."

"Fine," I sighed, knowing he was right. We needed answers, and me running off every time things got hard had to end. My brother needed me—and I was getting tired of pretending. "She's going to be pissed when she realizes I'm the one she took to bed last night. I should have told her who I was, but my cock drained all the blood from my brain."

"And what a glorious cock it is." Michael palmed my dick and grinned, trying to lighten the mood. "But relax. You're assuming she'll realize it was you. If she was as drunk as you say, she might not remember much about last night. Let's just take it as it comes, okay?" He cupped my cheek, his touch both comforting and stirring. "Trust me, Antonio."

I wanted to believe him, I did, but nothing ever went our way —ever. Not lately, anyway. I didn't think it was too much to ask for things to settle down. Massimo and Madison deserved to have their wedding, and Riley deserved to give birth without worrying about jail time. I looked at Michael, who was tugging on a shirt while watching me with those intense eyes that always seemed to see right through me. He made me feel things I never thought I'd feel, and the shame and guilt I held inside was ruining me—ruining our chance.

As if he could sense my turmoil, he stepped in front of me and pulled me against his chest. "Stop. You're doing it again. You're fighting this because of your false belief that your family will flip out. I know them, Antonio, and they will love you no matter what."

"I'm afraid, Michael." Resting my forehead against his, I sighed deeply. "I know you believe they'll be okay with my sexual orientation, but what if they aren't? And what about you? Aren't you the least bit worried they'll fire you as our legal team?" I stepped back and shook my head, feeling the weight of our complicated situation. "Let's not forget the fact I came here and slept with you after sleeping with Mia."

Michael's expression softened, and he placed his hands on my shoulders. "Antonio, I'm not worried about my job. I'm worried about you. About us. And as for Mia, we'll deal with that when the time comes. You didn't do anything wrong. We didn't do anything wrong. What matters now is figuring out who's behind all this and making sure everyone is safe."

I laughed at his ridiculous suggestion. Finding a woman who would accept us both was like finding a unicorn in the desert—it didn't exist. Even if we did find someone who wanted us both, she might not go for Michael and me having sex with each other. Then you add in the fact my family was the mafia. You could bet your ass any sane woman would hightail it far away from this twisted idea of a relationship.

"It doesn't matter. For now, we need to worry about clearing Riley's name and making sure Vin doesn't do something stupid in the meantime."

The sound of the doorbell interrupted our conversation.

"She's here." Michael smirked at me when my body stiffened. "Relax. We'll tell her we're friends, so it won't seem unusual for you to be here."

I followed him down the hallway to the door. Michael lived off the beaten path of the Vegas strip. His house was like Fort Knox, with a massive brick wall surrounding the property, set way off the main road. If someone had followed her here, he would know, since there was only one way in and one way out.

Michael opened the door and guided her inside. "Come on in, Mia."

"Wow, this is a beautiful place… kind of in the boonies, though."

He shut the door behind her. "Makes it easy to know if someone follows me home."

"Paranoid much?"

I smiled at her teasing tone.

Michael shrugged his shoulders. "I work for the Anastasi's." His gaze found mine, and he smirked. "The FBI aren't the only ones who hate them, Mia. You should know that."

"Yes. I do." She stepped around him and skidded to a stop when her eyes locked on me. "Antonio Anastasi. I didn't think I'd see you again."

I forced my expression to remain neutral as I greeted her. "Good morning, Miss Hill."

She rolled her eyes and stepped into the living room. "Please… lose the formalities. Me being here breaks the rules and then some. I don't think we need to keep up the professionalism act… don't you agree?"

"Right… Mia." My voice came out huskier than I meant, and I swear I saw a flash of recognition in her gaze.

Her eyes were the most unusual color, almost turquoise, and I couldn't look away. I hadn't noticed them last night when I had her pinned beneath me. Fuck, just thinking about her naked and splayed on the bed had my cock twitching in my pants. I blinked, coughing to cover the groan that almost slipped out, and turned around. Of course, it wasn't before catching Michael's knowing glance and his humorous smirk.

"Michael says you're being followed. I can assure you it's not my family."

Her footsteps padded across the hardwood floor. "How can you be so sure?"

I knew she'd expect proof but telling her would risk her finding out it was my cock buried between her thighs last night. "I would know."

"Why are you here." She squinted at me, her thoughts screaming in the pools of her eyes. I could swear recognition was tickling her memory, trying to rear its ugly head, ousting my secret.

I ignored her statement and sighed. "We need to figure out who is following you, because I am certain they're probably following my family."

"Right." Mia shook her head and turned to face Michael. "I brought the file. I'm breaking every oath I've taken and could get disbarred for this, but I believe Riley is innocent. So much so, I'm willing to stake my career and reputation on that, but I'm going to need something from you."

"What's that?" Michael stepped toward her, crowding her body against the back of the couch.

I watched in utter fascination as her body seemed to shake with need, the closer he got. Her throat bobbed when she swallowed, and I couldn't ignore the primal reaction it stirred in me.

She held her head up and held his gaze, "Why are they hard up for Vincenzo? The evidence points to Dmitri Ivanov as being the man in control of La Lama. What's his connection?"

Michael glanced my way before speaking. "He wants control of everything. Pinning La Lama's murders on Vincenzo would eliminate a problem for him. The Anastasis have fucked up his plans and taken something from him. He won't stop until he's sought revenge."

"So, this is all about revenge?" Her voice hitched when Michael reached out and brushed a loose strand of hair from her face.

It was like watching two magnets being drawn toward each other, and I couldn't tear my eyes away from the impending crash.

"Yes." Just as he was moving in to claim her lips, his phone rang. "Fuck." He shot me a look—one full of irritation coupled with need. He wanted her as much as I did, and that thought made my dick ramrod hard.

"Yes. He's here with me now. No—" His mouth snapped shut, and he nodded his head. "We'll meet you there." Michael pocketed his phone. "We have to go. Mia, call Agent Jackson."

Her head swiveled between us, her confusion matching my own. "Why, what happened?"

Michael glanced at me. His eyes were filled with pain as he spoke. "Vincenzo has been attacked. They are rushing him to the hospital as we speak."

I didn't think as I started toward the door, my heart pounding with fear.

"Slow down, Antonio." Michael grabbed my arm and held me firmly. "I'll drive."

"Where was he attacked?" Mia's expression was muddled with concern.

"He was leaving the restaurant, and someone attacked him. The person shoved a knife into the back of his throat and left him for dead." Michael held my arm, never breaking contact with me. "Do you believe me now, Mia? That this is bigger than anyone realizes?"

"I'll talk to the D.A." She started toward the door, a look of determination on her face. "These changes everything. I'll be in touch." Mia paused beside me and placed her hand on my chest. A strange look filled her eyes as she stared into my tear-laden gaze. "I'll pray for your brother."

I squeezed her hand, nodding my head as I pleaded with her. "End this shit with Riley. She can't deal with this, jail, and pregnancy."

"I'll do what I can."

I watched as she walked out and then turned to Michael. "Let's go. I can't lose him." He pulled me into his embrace and ran his hands through my hair.

"You won't." Michael pressed his lips to mine, the comfort of his touch warming me from the inside out. I couldn't keep hiding the way I felt about him. Not from myself or from my brothers. Once this was over, I'd come clean with everyone. Michael deserved that much from me.

"Oh…." Mia's shocked voice drew us apart. "I…" She shifted nervously at the door. "Forgot my bag."

"It's on the table." Michael pointed toward the coffee table, then watched as she moved into the living room. "Mia."

Michael stepped in front of the door, blocking her path. "I owe you some kind of explanation."

"You don't owe me anything."

"Stop." He grabbed her wrist gently. "We kissed, Mia, and seeing me kissing a man has to leave you with questions."

"It doesn't matter." She tried to tug free. "The kiss was a mistake… obviously."

"I'm bisexual," Michael blurted out, shocking both of us. "I'm attracted to men and women."

She blushed as she glanced at me. "And he's okay with that?"

"Yes, he's fine with it."

My brows knitted together in confusion that he didn't "out" me as being bisexual as well.

"I'm attracted to you, Mia. I know it's more than you want to hear, but I needed you to know the kiss meant something to me."

"What about him? That's kind of awful to him, isn't it?"

"Mia." My voice cracked. "I need to tell you something."

She turned toward me. "I don't need to know what your relationship with him is, Antonio. Again, it's not my business."

Michael nodded, silently begging me to tell her the truth.

"I know you're not being followed by my family because I've been watching you, and I didn't tell your boss about your meeting with Michael."

"What do you mean, you've been watching me?"

I held my breath. Everything was unraveling in front of my eyes at record speed, and I didn't know how to stop it or if I even wanted to.

"Well?" Her voice jerked me to the present.

"Look, I want to tell you everything, but I need to get to the hospital. Fuck." I ran my hands through my hair, frustrated with the timing of all this.

"Tell her, Antonio." Michael pressed his palm to my shoulder.

"Tell me what? For Christ's sake, you two are looney. I have to go." She shoved the bag up over her shoulder and pushed past Michael.

"It was me last night." My words halted her steps. "I was at your house last night dealing with the mess one of my men made..."

"It was you last night, what?" She searched my face, a moment of confusion, but as she searched her memory, the realization struck hard. "You were the man in my house last night. The man I..." Her voice trailed off. "Oh, fuck."

"I tried to leave, but you were adamant. I've wanted you from the moment I saw your picture. I think a part of me agreed to go undercover and watch you because I needed to get close to you... and not entirely for the reasons you think."

"You fucked me." She pointed her finger at me, then at Michael. "And you kissed me. Do you see how messed up this is?"

"It wasn't planned. You know that." Michael stepped behind her, his chest pressing against her back. "Deep down, you can't deny our attraction."

Mia's eyes closed as she took a deep breath. "It's wrong, Michael. I slept with an Anastasi. A man who's related to the woman I'm trying for manslaughter. Not to mention a man who just openly admitted to trying to get dirt on me for."

I stepped in front of her, hoping she'd felt the connection between us last night—the connection that was burning in the room now. "But how do you feel?"

"I…" She glanced up, licking her lips at my nearness. Her eyes flashed with confusion, and I watched as she stepped out from between us, clutching her bag to her chest. "I have to go."

Michael and I watched as she ran down the steps and jumped into her car, her vehicle disappearing down the drive before either of us spoke.

I exhaled. "I fucked everything up."

"No, you didn't. I know you feel it, so does she, but this is a lot right now. Hell, her career is about to implode, and she doesn't know how to handle that."

"What if she never talks to us again?" I turned to look at Michael.

"She will. Give her time." He leaned forward and pressed a chaste kiss to my lips. "Let's go. We need to see about

Vincenzo and Riley. This whole situation reeks of Dmitri Ivanov."

I nodded, feeling the gravity of our circumstances weighing heavily on my shoulders. We needed to get to the hospital, to be there for Vincenzo and figure out our next steps. As we drove through the city, the tension between us was palpable, but Michael's hand on mine was a small comfort.

Michael squeezed my hand as we stood by Vincenzo's bedside. "He's strong, Antonio. He'll pull through."

I nodded, though my heart felt heavy. "We need to find out who did this and make them pay."

"We will," Michael promised, his voice low and fierce. "But right now, we need to be there for him."

The stakes were higher than ever, and the lines between personal and professional had blurred beyond recognition. But as I looked at Michael, his unwavering support gave me the strength I needed to face whatever came next.

Together, we would find the truth and protect those we cared about, no matter what the cost.

six

MIA

SOMETHING WAS COMPLETELY AMISS. Who stabbed Vincenzo, and how the hell did I sleep with an Anastasi and not know it? The rhythmic sound of my fingers rolling across the steering wheel kept me anchored to the present. An overwhelming need to go to the hospital had me squirming like a child in my seat. Going there would be an epic mistake—not just for me, but for everyone involved. Before I could explore my feelings for either man, I needed to clear Riley's name. Her innocence was becoming more certain than the green light currently signaling me safely through the intersection. My thumb pressed the call button on my steering wheel, the automated voice demanding who to call.

"Call Donovan."

Patience was not a virtue I currently had. Between the weight of my foot and the grip on the leather circle in front of me, I was certain my driving was equivalent to a sixteen-year-old with a brand-new license. It felt like the phone rang for an eternity before his voice finally filled the cab of my car.

"Hill, this better be worth interrupting my Saturday for."

"Vincenzo Anastasi has been stabbed. They're rushing him to the hospital as we speak."

"What?" Him being shocked was an understatement. "How?"

"Not sure." I tapped the edge of my steering wheel. "Should I go to the hospital to see if I can get any details?"

"Fuck. Where are you on evidence with the Lawson woman?"

"There is none." I was done pretending there was.

"Bullshit." He growled into the phone. "Like I told you yesterday, find something."

"What do you want me to do? Conjure up something? She's innocent and you know it." I spat back, irritated he wasn't listening to what I'd been saying for weeks.

"Then call Agent Jackson and tell him that yourself. I told you, the feds are breathing down my neck on this one. They're threatening to take over this case if we don't wrap it up soon."

His words filled me with utter disgust. Being pushed around by anyone was not my thing. If calling the agent handling the case on the feds side ended this, then I would take one for the team.

"I'll call him. I'm done digging up shit that isn't there."

"Are you willing to risk your career on this, Mia?" It was never a good sign when he used my first name.

As the district attorney, he kept things at the utmost professional level possible. Calling me by my given name was a bad thing, but he was right. This would change my career in a way I wasn't sure I was ready for, but in my gut, I knew what I had to do. In my mind, I could see it clearly. I was standing on the tracks with nowhere to go, and the train was speeding toward me with no chance of stopping. I thought of my parents and what they would do in my position, and I knew instantly what I needed to say.

"Yes."

"Fine. Do what you think is best." The silence inside the car was deafening.

I ended the call with Donovan and immediately dialed the judge presiding over the case. The phone rang only twice before his gruff voice answered.

As the car edged forward in traffic, I knew this was the tipping point for not only my career, but my life. For so long, I'd felt like an empty vessel drifting in a turbulent ocean with no direct course to shore. Now… now I felt a weight lift off my shoulders. I pulled my car into the parking lot of the emergency room after driving there without realizing it.

"You are really starting to annoy me," the judge growled into the line.

"There's been an incident that will fuck us over… excuse the language."

He grumbled, obviously, over my theatrics. "I am starting to think your demands are just a delay tactic."

"I understand why you would think that, but Vincenzo Anastasi was stabbed and is currently in the emergency room."

"I am sure a man like him is used to being stabbed."

"In the neck?" I paused, waiting to hear what comment he might have after that tidbit.

"Fuck."

"Exactly. With Riley pregnant, and now this, I think the trial can wait. Plus, it gives us time to connect the missing dots. I'm calling Agent Jackson in a moment to compare notes. This attack was not a coincidence."

"I don't suppose it was." He huffed a frustrated sigh. "Fine. I'll push it out indefinitely. Going to trial while a pregnant woman's husband is near dead doesn't look good for this department, anyway. Let me know if something changes."

I hung up, relieved I had more time to put this mess to bed.

The sky was a brilliant blue, the kind of sky that normally makes you feel elated and happy to be alive. But that was the furthest thing I was feeling. Tiny tendrils of fear were pumping through my veins, paralyzing me in my car. I watched the people come and go from the entrance as I stared out the window from inside my vehicle.

The tapping at my driver-side window made me jump like a startled bird.

"Mia?"

An anxious breath hissed out of my lungs when I saw Michael standing beside my car. "Jesus. Michael, you scared the shit out of me."

"Unlock your doors." Like a big cat stalking his prey, Michael eased around the hood of my car and slipped in beside me. "Are you okay? You looked lost sitting in your car."

You could say that." My eyes closed as I dropped my head to the seat's headrest. "I called the judge."

"Why?" Michael turned to face me, his enormous frame taking up the entire front seat. "You already got your delay."

"I wanted him to know what was happening. With this…" I motioned toward the hospital. "I wanted to give Riley time. I'm not a monster, you know?"

Michael watched me, his gaze boring into mine. He said nothing and everything, just sitting there in silence. I fidgeted beneath his scrutinizing gaze, shifting my eyes nervously.

"I know. Look…" Michael sighed. "This was an intentional hit. Agent Jackson came by and showed us something they had collected from the scene. Dmitri Ivanov did this, Mia."

"Are you sure?"

"He left his calling card."

My head pounded with this additional information. If Dmitri Ivanov was the one who stabbed Vincenzo, we would have bigger problems on our hands than this case with Riley. Dmitri was at the top of the wanted list for the FBI and Interpol. He was wanted for a laundry list of shit I couldn't comprehend.

"I don't know how, but Riley won't go to jail."

Michael tilted his head in question. "How can you promise us that?"

"I'm going to point a giant spotlight on Dmitri Ivanov… smear his name in the media and make him slip up again. This time we'll be waiting."

"That's too dangerous. I can't let you do that. This man tried to kill his own daughter. You'd be like a bump in the road to him. A bug he'll squash with the bottom of his shoe. Do you understand?"

"Get out of my car, Mr. Brighton." The rage I felt in my blood at his dismissal of my ability to handle myself was beyond anything I'd ever felt. If Michael thought he could tell me how to operate, he had another thing coming. A fragile doll, I was not—and he would soon learn that. "Let your client know the trial has been delayed indefinitely. I assume I don't have to worry about her fleeing the country since her husband is lying in a hospital bed, right?"

"Why are you doing this? Mia…"

"Move. Now." The warmth of his body sent shock waves through my core as I leaned across him and shoved the door open. "Let me know if he dies. That would change things." I hated being so callous with my words, but I was tired of being told how to handle things.

Michael's hesitation poured from him like a broken faucet leaking water. He took a deep breath and nodded before slipping out of the seat.

"Don't do something that will put you at risk."

"Good day," I called out as the door slammed shut. I pulled off, leaving a bewildered man in my wake. I watched in the rearview mirror as Michael shoved his hands in his pockets and stared after me. His form grew smaller in the tiny rectangle as I navigated away from him.

I was done playing nice. If she wasn't guilty, I would figure it out and end this game—and maybe, take down one of the most notorious criminals in the world.

Dmitri Ivanov didn't know who he was messing with.

I was done playing nice. If Riley wasn't guilty, I would figure it out and end this game—and maybe, take down one of the most notorious criminals in the world.

Dmitri Ivanov didn't know who he was messing with.

Determined, I drove home with a newfound sense of purpose. The usual apprehension had vanished, replaced by a steely resolve. I arrived at my apartment and went straight to my home office, flipping open my laptop and immersing myself in research. Dmitri Ivanov had a vast network, but no one was untouchable. His arrogance would be his undoing.

I sifted through articles, legal documents, and surveillance reports, piecing together the intricate web of his operations. The more I learned, the clearer it became: Dmitri had made enemies on every side. He operated with a mix of brutality and cunning, but he wasn't infallible. His overconfidence left a trail, and I was determined to follow it to its bitter end.

seven

MICHAEL

RED-HOT BLISTERING ANGER—THAT'S what I felt as Mia tore out of the hospital parking lot. She had no clue what she was poking at, and nothing I could do would prepare her for the swarm of hornets she would get when she agitated the monster. Dmitri Ivanov was not a man to trifle with. He'd left a trail of blood and death in his path of destruction, and she was crazy if she thought, by some miracle, she was immune to his savage ways. Hell, Vincenzo was proof of that—even if she didn't really know who he was. I did. He was La Lama, a fucking nightmare by all accounts, and was currently lying in a bed, clinging to life by a worn-out thread.

"Michael?" Antonio's voice cut through my haze of red. "I—" His voice cracked as he shook back the tears threatening to fall.

I gripped his shoulder and looked him in the eyes. "Hey, Vin's going to be okay. He's the toughest prick I know." I started toward where we parked. "Let's go back to my place and talk. I need to bring you up to speed on some things, and this isn't the place to do it."

He paused, glancing over his shoulder at the entry. "I should stay."

"No, you shouldn't. Riley is the only one they'll let inside with him, and Massimo promised to keep you apprised of any changes. All you can do now is pray and be there when Riley needs you."

Antonio nodded, moving on autopilot as I guided him across the parking lot to my awaiting vehicle. The last twenty-four hours had been a roller coaster of emotions. His sudden appearance at my door last night had thrown me for a loop. When I told him months ago that I would wait for him, I meant it. The connection I felt with him wasn't a passing phase. It was deep and real and something I knew I wouldn't find with just anyone. I just needed him to see it as well—and he did, but his fear blocked the path to having what he wanted. Even more confusing, we shared an attraction to the same woman. A woman who, by all rights, should've been off-limits to both of us, but by some turn of luck, Antonio had slept with her. It wasn't planned, and he tried to do the right thing, but she was a demanding little vixen. One of the many traits we were both attracted to. As much as I wanted her in my bed, Antonio needed my focus right now. He was the sensitive one in the family—the one who wore his feelings on his sleeve—and this incident would haunt him for some time.

Only the sound of the music filled the inside of our ride home. His sadness washed over me like a rainstorm in April. Pulling down my driveway, I glanced at his profile. The lines on his face seemed to have grown deeper and bolder in the last few hours, aging him in a short amount of time. I knew from talking to Massimo that their parents were due in from Sicily by morning. For now, all he had was me, and I planned to take care of him—no matter his state of mind or how he tried to push me away.

"Hey." I pressed my palm to his knee. "We're here."

Antonio's eyes seemed to be unfocused as he stared out the windshield. I could tell he wasn't hearing me, lost in his own head. The seatbelt smacked the door frame as I unlatched it and stepped out. The day had slipped through our fingers, and the sun was high in the sky, mocking us from behind the clouds. I helped him from the car, my heart aching for the man I'd fallen in love with a month ago. I'd never seen Antonio like this. Even though he was least likely to exert violence, he was still hardened to the life his family lived. Right now, at this moment, it was like looking at a little boy searching for the comfort of his mother.

"Why?" Antonio finally whispered.

"I don't know."

The lock clicking into place seemed to snap Antonio back to the present.

"We're at your house?"

"Yeah. You're going to stay here with me until this mess blows over. I've already called Madison—she's going to bring some stuff over."

His face scrunched up in confusion. "You called Madison?"

"I know you two are close. I figured she would be cool with this."

Antonio cocked a brow at me. "This?" His tired eyes challenged me to say more.

"Yes, this." I took a calming breath. "Stop fucking around and go sit down. I'll fix you a drink. I think you've earned one. Plus—" I tossed my keys on the entry table, "I need to tell you about my conversation with Mia. I think you'll need some whiskey to hear what I have to say."

"Great. Something else to fuck with my day." Antonio flung himself down on the couch and sank into the cushions.

"Great. Something else to fuck with my day." Antonio flung himself down on the couch and sank into the cushions.

I couldn't help but chuckle at his childlike behavior. Even if it was warranted, it was ridiculous to watch. The decanter of whiskey gleamed in the kitchen light. The amber liquid shined through the glass bottle, begging to be poured. I filled two glasses and carried them, along with the bottle, to the living room. Antonio had his head pressed against the back of the couch, staring at the ceiling, his hands fused in his hair.

"I hate Dmitri. If I could bury a blade between his ribs, I would. He's taken so much from my family. First Madison… then me. And let's not forget Katya, his own daughter. Plus, Krissy and Megan. They were just employees who didn't deserve to be sucked into this madness." Dmitri had done some serious damage to the family.

Killing Krissy instead of Madison, then kidnapping Antonio had rocked the family hard. And if that wasn't enough damage, he killed Megan, one of Vincenzo's longtime servers. It had been a warning to back off, but it enraged Vin, which was exactly what Dmitri wanted. Only, it was Donat Ivanov Vincenzo killed weeks later.

The fucked-up part was Riley taking the fall. She had been working as an undercover agent with the FBI, and falling in love with Vincenzo pushed her to protect him. Now, she was pregnant and awaiting trial. Vincenzo had to pull through this. I wasn't sure the family could come back from his death.

I handed Antonio a glass and sat beside him, the weight of the past weeks heavy on both our shoulders.

"Fuck. I don't like how this is starting."

"Promise me." I held his gaze. "Hear me out, then we will figure out what to do."

"Fine. What could be worse than my brother on his deathbed?"

"Mia wants to go after Dmitri," I began, watching Antonio's reaction carefully. "She thinks she can expose him, make him slip up, and bring him down."

His eyes darkened as his grip tightened around the glass. "She's playing with fire, Michael. Dmitri won't hesitate to kill her." Antonio sat up, his senses coming back to him.

"She is tired of playing games and knows he's behind everything. Mia is under the misguided impression if she makes him mad enough, he'll slip up."

"And you didn't tell her that was suicide?"

"I did. She pushed me out of her car and drove off."

"Fuck." Antonio stood. "She doesn't know who she's fucking with. Call Agent Jackson. He needs to know she's going to get herself killed."

My phone rang as if on cue, and Agent Jackson's face lit up on the screen. I shared a troubled glance with Antonio as I hit the speaker button.

"We were just talking about you."

"We have a problem. The D.A. just held a press conference."

"Let me guess." I looked at Antonio. "He just tied Dmitri Ivanov to Vincenzo's stabbing and Riley's arrest."

"Yep. This is going to get ugly, boys. I know the family has their own security. Now would be a good time to amp it up. I'll put an agent at the hospital, but the rest of the family is at risk."

"What about the prosecutor?"

"It's up to the district attorney's office to ensure she is protected, but the D.A. just painted a huge target on their backs. I tried calling Miss Hill, but she didn't answer. I'll keep trying, but this just became bigger than Riley. Be ready." The phone went black, making my phone feel like a dead weight in my palm.

Without thinking, I tried calling Mia. "Fuck."

"This is fucked up, Michael. Why did she do this?"

"She knows Riley is innocent, and maybe she thought this was the only way to clear her name."

"Call her again." Just like before, her voicemail picked up.

A couple of hours had passed, and the sky was dimming into darkness. There was no way she was still driving.

"Surely, she made it home by now. Why is she still not

answering?" Antonio paced the floor. "What if something happened? Dmitri moves fast."

"Calm down. Let's give her a little more time and try again. If she hasn't answered or called us back in a bit, we'll do something."

Antonio continued to pace the floor like a wild animal. "This is fucked up."

The pain of today was taking its toll on him, making him act irrationally. Hell, I was even starting to feel the stress of today's events. The Anastasi family was one of the most powerful families in Vegas and Italy. If they hadn't been able to bring Dmitri down yet, Mia didn't stand a chance.

"Michael, I can't just sit here," Antonio insisted, his voice tinged with desperation. He pushed to his feet, "Wait—the cameras. Let me check the feed and then we can decide what to do."

Neither of us was prepared for what we saw.

eight

MIA

THE MOMENT I pulled into my driveway, I knew something was wrong. It wasn't an obvious thing, more like a gut feeling. You know the one. The sensation you get right before the scary moment happens in the movie. Every hair on my neck was standing at attention, warning me to stay in the car—but I didn't. My door was ajar, and the lights were on inside my house. With as much sleuth as I could muster, I pushed open the front door and stepped inside. Everything appeared to be in its place, making me wonder if I'd just forgotten to pull the door shut all the way when I'd left earlier. After inspecting every room, I headed upstairs to investigate the rest of the house. Much like the bottom floor, it was untouched. Maybe the wind pushed it open—if only there had been wind today. Someone was trying to scare me, and I had my suspicions about who.

Because of the brief press conference my boss held, a giant target was now aimed at my head. And if I was right, Dmitri Ivanov was to blame for this entire mess, and Riley was a victim of circumstance. I wasn't about to put her in jail if that was true. As I was searching my room for anything missing, a loud crash outside made me jump. Just as I tiptoed to the window to peer out, my power went out, bathing the house in darkness. Someone was in my driveway, tampering with my car. My cell phone vibrated in my pocket, jerking my attention from the window. It was Michael again. He'd tried calling many times, but I hadn't wanted to talk to him.

"Michael?" I whispered into the phone, my eyes searching outside again.

"Mia." Michael's voice filtered through the device. "You're in danger."

"Obviously. Someone's outside my house."

"Don't move. Antonio is headed your way. Why didn't your boss put a detail on your house? Doesn't he know what trouble he's brought to you both?"

"I—" My breath caught as the distinct sound of my front door being kicked in made me freeze.

"Mia… what's wrong?"

"Someone's inside," I whispered into the phone, sliding down onto the floor as I spoke. I eased myself under my bed, flattening my body as much as I could. "I shouldn't have come inside. The door was open… I-I think someone had already been in here."

"I'm calling the police." Michael's voice was bordering on panicked.

"No. Please. Don't hang up." I closed my eyes and tried to calm my breathing. "Isn't Antonio coming?" As if on cue, I heard shouting and scuffling downstairs. "I hear shouting. What if—" A gunshot rang out, making me whimper.

"Mia?" Michael barked into the phone. "Talk to me, Mia. Was that a gunshot?"

"Yes." I couldn't control the sobs any longer. If someone was here, there was no way they wouldn't hear me. "Why is this happening to me? Oh God, they're coming up the stairs."

"Mia." My bedroom door burst in, revealing a very pissed-off Antonio inside the doorway.

"Antonio!" I cried out, pushing myself from under my hiding spot. "He's here." I sobbed harder as Antonio wrapped his arms around me, pulling me close. He pulled the phone from my hand.

"Call Massimo. There's a body I need removed. Yes, she's fine. We'll be there soon." He pocketed my phone and held my shoulders as he looked me over.

"What do you mean, there's a body?"

"I shot a man downstairs." He turned from me and went into my closet, returning with my suitcase. "Pack in this. We've gotta go."

"Antonio." I folded my arms across my chest. "Did you hear yourself? There's a dead man in my house. A man you shot. We have to call the police."

"And tell them what? Antonio Anastasi killed a man. They'll throw me in the cell quicker than you can say guilty. The moment your boss outed Dmitri, you made yourself vulnerable. He'll kill you, Mia. That dead man downstairs? That's why he was here. Do you understand now? Dmitri Ivanov is a sick man who will stop at nothing to have his way. This isn't a game. Now, pack."

I stared at him as he started pulling things from my drawers and tossing them on the bed. If I went with him, I would be forfeiting my career. But if I didn't, I was sealing my fate for death. Hurrying into my closet, I pulled down whatever I could grab, carried them to the bed, and tossed them in the massive case he had opened. It was like I was floating in space, watching myself move around from above. After I shoved everything I could inside the bag, I pulled it off the bed, then stood, frozen in a trance.

"Come on." Antonio grabbed the bag from me, laced his fingers in mine, and headed out the door. "Someone will be here soon to take care of him. Don't look." He wrapped his arm around me and shielded me from the carnage lying on my living room floor. "I promise I'll protect you, Mia."

My mind must have blanked out, taking me to a space that blocked out the world, because I didn't remember Antonio putting me in the car. It was an all too familiar place, one I had visited in my head when my parents died. It kept me safe —even if only temporarily. The soft rhythmic sound of the tires beating against the pavement seemed to lull me into a false sense of peace.

"Mia."

Antonio's voice sounded miles away as I blinked through the haze shrouding my eyes and saw the familiar sight of Michael's house. The brick wall blocked out the rest of the world, creating a haven away from the evil waiting beyond the desert's sanctuary. He rounded the car and opened my door.

"Come on. Let's go inside." He wrapped his fingers around my arm, guiding me up the steps and into the foyer. "She's in shock."

My ears heard him, but my eyes wouldn't focus. I was caught in between a nightmare and real life. What had I done? My career would be over once my boss learned where I was. And if he fired me, Riley would be at the FBI's mercy when they took over the case. I buried my face in my hands and let the tears out.

"Hey." Michael sat down on the couch beside me, his arm wrapped around me. "We're going to fix this, Mia."

"How?" I looked up, noticing Antonio sat on my other side. "I've fucked up and now…" I took a deep breath and blew it out. "What am I going to do?" Michael pulled me against his side and held me as I cried. "I did this. I should have listened to you, but I thought it would help Riley," I mumbled against his shirt.

"Maybe you were right. Maybe this is exactly what we need to make Dmitri slip up." Antonio rubbed my back, his palm moving in circles over my shirt. "Don't blame yourself. Riley will be fine as long as Vincenzo pulls through." His voice cracked at the mention of his brother.

"Oh God." My gaze sought him out. "Here I am crying, and your brother is lying in the hospital, fighting for his life."

"It's okay." Antonio reached up and fingered the strands of hair that had fallen from my ponytail. "He's tough, and if I know my brother, he isn't going to miss the birth of my niece and nephew. Right now, we need to come up with a plan. You can't go home, Mia. I know you think you can handle this alone, but the safest place for you is here, where Michael and I can protect you."

The weight of his words pressed down on me, and I realized the truth in them. I couldn't face this alone. The stakes were too high, and Dmitri was too dangerous. But it still made no sense—and I knew I'd be risking more than my career. "You want me to stay here?" I glanced around the room. "What will I tell my boss?"

"The truth." Michael stood. "Tell him you are working with us to prove Riley's innocence and help bring down Dmitri. Agent Jackson believes us… so make your boss believe in us as well."

"I'll call him in the morning." A massive yawn escaped my lips. "I just want to go to sleep."

Michael stood and held his hand out. "Let me show you where you'll be sleeping."

"What about you two?" I looked back at Antonio.

"There's enough room in my house for both of you. I'd rather it be that way. My place is hidden and has top-notch security. If someone comes on my property, we'll know."

I nodded, still overwhelmed with emotions I didn't understand.

Michael's hand was warm against mine as he led me upstairs. His place was like something out of a *Better Homes and Gardens* magazine. It was a two-story cabin, but with all the modern luxuries. There were three doors, which I assumed led to bedrooms. When Michael opened the first door, I was completely taken aback. It was beautiful. A massive bed, covered in hues of gray and black linens, filled one of the walls. On the opposite side sat an ornate wood dresser. The wood was stained in a gray hue, giving the room a regal vibe.

"Wow, this is gorgeous."

"This will be your room while you're here." He smiled and pointed to the door across from mine. "That's Antonio's and mine is next to his. You have your own bathroom as well. There are towels in the cabinet and toiletries inside the stall. If you need anything at all, just ask."

"Can I see them?"

He nodded, leading me across the hall as Antonio stood leaned against the wall, watching us.

"This is where Antonio is staying. The bathroom joins our rooms. And this—" he stepped through the massive bathroom in between the rooms and into an even more stunning space, "is mine."

"Wow. This…" I smiled. "Your home is magnificent, Michael. Thank you for letting me stay here."

"We're going to protect you, Mia. I promise." He pressed his fingers beneath my chin and peered into my eyes. "Nothing is going to hurt you. Not Dmitri. Not being here. Do you understand?"

"Yes," I whispered, my heart beating a mile a minute. "I should shower."

Michael stepped back, letting me turn and head into the room alone. My bag was on the bed. Antonio had obviously carried it up for me. I didn't know what was going to happen, but I had a feeling it was going to be explosive—for everyone.

nine

ANTONIO

WATCHING Michael with Mia was pure torture. Not because I was jealous—the opposite, in fact. The two of them together made me hope for things I still believed impossible. Hell, Mia still hadn't accepted it was me she'd slept with, then she learned Michael and I had been together as well. She didn't seem put out by it, simply confused. I could tell she was attracted to both of us, and that seemed to scare her. I think what frightened her more was the potential risk of losing her job for staying with us.

"You think she'll be okay?" Michael sat down on his bed and watched me in the doorway. His brows were furrowed, and his eyes held a deep, almost palpable worry. His lips were pressed into a thin line, and the usual lightness in his expression was replaced by a heavy, anxious look. He seemed lost in thought, the weight of the situation clearly reflected in every tense line and shadow on his face.

"I'd give my life to make sure of it." My tone was filled with determination. "She didn't deserve this. Dmitri needs to die."

"I couldn't agree more." Michael laid back, staring at the ceiling. "I like her."

The bed dipped as I laid down beside him. "Me, too." I laced my fingers with his, seeking comfort in the touch. "I'm worried about Vin and Riley."

Michael rolled onto his side, his blue eyes softening as he smiled. "He's tough."

"I should tell Massimo about us. I'm tired of hiding. It's exhausting." My lips pressed into his knuckles, the need for honesty weighing heavily on me... "Do you think it's wrong, with Vin in the hospital and with everything going on?"

"Massimo loves you, Antonio. I don't think he'll care. If you want to tell him, then we will. If you don't, we'll wait."

Michael leaned down and pressed his lips to mine. Our mouths fused together as his tongue slipped inside, exploring the depths. His body rolled, covering mine as he deepened the kiss. It was wrong to be lost in each other with Mia in the other room, but we couldn't deny the passion we felt for one another.

"Oh." Mia's gasp caused us to pull apart, guilt flashing through me. "I just… never mind." She turned to leave, but I called out to her, desperation in my voice.

"Stop, Mia. Don't run. *Please.*"

Michael rolled onto the mattress and propped himself on his elbow, his gaze steady and inviting. "Come here."

Mia stood frozen, staring at our entwined legs. Her eyes flickered with confusion, but beneath that, there was unmistakable desire. Her breathing was shallow, and her eyes dilated as she found me staring at her.

"I should go." She didn't make any attempts to move.

"I think you should stay." My voice pleaded with her. "I know you feel it, Mia. What are you afraid of?"

"*Everything*," she whispered, her head turning to look away. "You don't understand."

"Then tell us. We want you... we won't hide that fact. Are you bothered by the fact we're together?"

"No." Her head jerked in our direction, and she blinked. "I was in a similar relationship once..." She paused, her eyes clouding over as if she was lost in a memory. "If you can call it that. It didn't end well, but that's not the problem."

"Then what's the problem?" Michael asked, his voice soft, yet coaxing.

"I'm supposed to be putting your family in jail."

"Is that what you want to do?" I watched as the myriad of emotions crossed her face. I didn't care what she said. I wanted to know what she felt. If she wanted us as much as we wanted her, the rest was just noise. "Because I don't think you do."

"I don't." She looked down at her feet again. "I've felt so alone for the last few years. I thought coming here would help end that, and it didn't until—" She stopped herself.

"Until what?" My body moved from the bed, inching closer to her. "Say it, Mia."

I crowded her against the door, my palms pressed against the wood, creating a barrier she couldn't escape.

"I…" She swallowed hard as my knee wedged between her thighs, pressing against her center. She groaned, arching her chest into mine, her body betraying her internal conflict.

"Say *it,*" I demanded. I needed to hear her say the words, just as much as she needed to say them. I knew she was fighting herself for wanting us—that needed to end tonight.

"You. Until you. And it's wrong on every level, but until you…and Michael—" Her eyes flicked to him. "I felt hollow. When Michael kissed me that night, for a moment, I forgot what it was like to be alone. He made me feel, and that scared me. Then you happened, and everything I thought I was supposed to do was demolished."

"What do you want?" The heat of my breath brushed against her neck, making her shiver.

"I don't know."

"I think you do. Michael." I called out to him, beckoning him from the bed. "You know exactly what you want—you only need to reach out and take it. Don't be afraid, Mia. We'll be there to catch you when you fall."

Michael stepped behind me and ran his hand down her cheek, his touch gentle yet commanding.

"We need to hear you say it, baby. Antonio and I want you… together, and if that's not something you can deal with, tell us now. But if it is, he and I will worship you like no one ever has."

"This could blow up in our faces." She glanced between the two of us, her teeth sinking into her lower lip as her palm came up to cup my cheek. "You know that, right?"

I leaned into her touch, desperate for more. "We'll deal with that when it happens. Right now, we want you. Can you handle that?"

She nodded, but I needed more. "No, baby. Words." I held my breath, waiting for her to give in.

"I can handle it," she finally said, her voice a soft but resolute whisper.

Wrapping my arms around her, I lifted her from the floor. Her legs instinctively wrapped around my waist as I pressed my mouth to hers. It felt like floating in a sea of clouds where the air was pure and beautiful. Michael rubbed my back, his lips kissing a trail of heat down my neck as I claimed Mia's lips.

Spinning her, I carried her to the bed and gently tossed her onto the mattress. Michael grabbed my neck and tugged my lips against his, the intensity of his kiss sending a shiver down my spine. He pulled my shirt off and tossed it to the floor, revealing the heat between us.

I smiled at Mia, who watched us with a blazing heat burning in her eyes. She propped herself up on her elbows, her gaze flicking between Michael and me, filled with both desire and anticipation.

"You're beautiful," I murmured, moving toward her, feeling Michael's presence close behind me.

Michael's hand slid around my waist, his fingers trailing over my skin as we approached the bed. Together, we leaned over Mia, our combined warmth surrounding her. I kissed her again, deep, and slow, savoring the taste of her, while Michael's hands explored her body, making her shiver beneath us.

"Are you sure?" Michael cocked an eyebrow at Mia, who lay on the bed still clothed in leggings and a cotton tee.

"Yes." Her voice was breathy but firm.

With a determined motion, she tugged the fabric over her head and threw it in a heap on the floor beside our clothes. Then, rolling over to her knees, she leaned forward and claimed Michael's mouth, her kiss hungry and passionate. Her hand wrapped around my shaft, sending a surge of pleasure through me.

I grunted in pleasure as she ran her palm up and down, her thumb smoothing the bead of cum around the tip, sending shivers of ecstasy through me. Michael's hands roamed her back, his fingers tracing the lines of her spine, making her arch and moan into his mouth.

"*Fuck.*" I groaned, my voice thick with need.

I groaned as my fingers tugged her hair free of the elastic holding it in place, letting her blonde tresses fall around her shoulders. Lost in a haze of lust, I closed my eyes and leaned back. Michael stood and latched onto my neck, licking, and sucking as Mia jacked me off.

Michael broke the kiss, his eyes dark with desire as he watched her hand work me. "You're incredible, Mia," he murmured, his voice a mix of admiration and lust. "Get her pants off," Michael growled against my mouth.

As I stepped away from their entangled bodies, I pushed her to her back onto the bed. I tugged the black fabric off her body, taking her panties with them. Michael stood naked, his cock red and swollen, begging for attention as he ran his palms across her smooth skin. I couldn't stop myself from dropping to my knees and swallowing his cock into my mouth.

"Jesus," Michael grunted as I bobbed my head and gripped his strong legs in my palms. "Antonio. Christ." He hissed as his dick hit the back of my throat.

I glanced at Mia out of the corner of my eye, as I sucked him off. My mouth broke into a grin around Michael's shaft when I saw his hand dip between her thighs. Michael was pressing his fingers between her cleft as I took my fill of him. His eyes closed as he gave into the sensations of my mouth on him and the warmth of her pussy as he fingered her.

"Stop. I don't want to come this way." He stepped out of my reach and jerked me to my feet.

My fingers found their way to Mia as I traced her nipple, tweaking the stiff peaks as I palmed her breast. Michael dropped to his knees between her legs and buried his face in her pussy. Mia cried out, her body writhing like a woman on fire as he devoured her core like a starving man.

"What do you want, baby?" I whispered in her ear as my finger pressed against the swollen pearl between her legs.

"Fuck me, someone… please."

Locking eyes with Michael, I nodded. He'd yet felt the warmth of her pussy, and I wanted him to have that chance. He grabbed a box of condoms and tossed one onto the bed. The tiny foil packet glistened in the soft light, begging me to wrap it around his cock. Tearing it open with my teeth, I rolled the barrier over his hard member, squeezing as I did. Michael groaned, his body jerking beneath my touch. Gripping him in my palm, I lined his shaft up with her sopping-wet center.

"Fuck her hard, Michael." I bit down on my lip as he pressed inside her.

His cock disappearing between her folds was one of the hottest things I'd ever seen. Mia groaned when he seated himself fully inside her channel.

"You like that? You like it when he sticks his cock inside you?" My thumb pressed against her swollen nub again, watching as he moved in and out. The sound of their bodies had me hard as a rock. I fisted my dick and jerked my palm along my shaft.

Mia turned her head, her palm covering mine. "Let me." She whispered as her fingers reached out and gripped my rod.

I moved closer and nearly died when she covered my mushroom head with her pouty lips. "Goddamn." I grunted, my hips thrusting forward on their own.

Her mouth worked my shaft like it was made for her as Michael fucked her. It felt like heaven, but I wanted to cum inside one of them. When I pulled out of her mouth, Mia whimpered as her first orgasm hit. "Oh God, Michael!"

Her body shattered around his cock as she cried out through the aftershocks of her release... "Please. I want to feel you both." Her fingers clawed at me, begging me to join the fray.

I blinked, shocked at her demand. I'd known she had a hidden kinky side from the pictures I'd seen, but I was still stunned at her request.

"You want me to fuck you while he's in you?"

"Yes." She moaned as he continued to stroke her walls. "Please."

"You heard the lady." Michael's body was covered in a sheen of sweat. He pulled out, forcing her to move over to give him space on the bed. He laid down and pulled her over him so she was straddling his legs. "Are you sure you want this?"

"Yes." She gripped his shaft in her palm and slid down over his cock. "I want you both."

I grabbed a condom and fished around in the drawer for lube. Once I found it, I coated myself in the clear jelly. My fingers massaged her backside, coating her hole to prepare her for my dick. She rocked against Michael's shaft as my finger slipped past the tight ring.

"Oh God," Mia groaned, her body shuddered as she rode him with my finger buried inside her ass.

Withdrawing my finger, I gripped her hips. "You ready, baby?"

She nodded, and Michael gave me a heated look that sizzled inside my veins. I had no doubt he was just as turned on as I was.

Slowly, I pressed my bulbous head into her backside. It was tight, but once I got past her bodies initial resistance, it felt like heaven. Michael's cock was hard against the thin barrier between our dicks, and his balls pressed against mine as I seated myself fully. She leaned forward and laced her fingers with his.

I began to move, causing her nipples to rub against Michael's chest. He moved his hips, thrusting in as I pulled out. The sensation was electric, sending a million volts of electricity through my veins. Sounds of sex filled the room as we raced toward a cliff we would never come back from. This moment would define us forever—with no hope of salvation.

"Oh, God!" Mia screamed out, her walls clamping down on Michael's shaft at the same time her tiny hole clenched around my dick...

I could feel Michael's cock as it swelled against mine, and his seed erupted inside her. My own release rushed out of me, making me lightheaded as I pumped into her, filling my own condom with cum. The rubbers ballooned with our desire, threatening to burst as Mia's body convulsed around us. At that moment, our souls morphed into one, binding us together permanently.

I don't know who moved first, but soon Mia was in the center of the bed, her body flush from our lovemaking. Michael had disposed of his condom and crawled beside her, his touch gentle and reassuring. I stripped off mine and tossed it into the trashcan beside the bed, then crawled into the space behind her. Her leg draped over mine as Michael's arm laid across both of our sides, creating a cocoon of warmth and security.

No words were needed; everything that could be said had been expressed through the coupling of our bodies. The connection we shared in those moments transcended any need for language. We fell into a deep slumber, a mess of tangled limbs and blankets, our breathing steady and synchronized.

Tomorrow was unknown, but right then, I knew Mia and Michael were mine. The night had forged a bond between us, one that felt both exhilarating and fragile. I only hoped that when the morning light shined, regret didn't follow. The weight of the world outside our sanctuary could wait; for now, we had each other, and that was enough.

MIA

THE HOT BODIES wrapped around mine were another reminder of how much I'd fucked up. The stale scent of sex and masculinity assaulted my senses as I inhaled a deep breath. I couldn't blame anyone but myself for what happened. I wanted last night just as much as they did.

They…

I was in bed with two men. Two vastly different men at that. Michael was an attorney who fought for the underdog, and Antonio… he was everything I stood against in my career. He was a criminal, untouchable by any law enforcement agency. His family was one of the most powerful in Vegas and Italy. And he was currently tangled up with me in another man's bed.

Blinking away the sleep, I slowly wiggled my way down to the end of the bed. They were knocked out from the exhaustion the night before had left them in. A night that had me sore in places that hadn't been touched in an awfully long time. My movement jostled Michael, causing him to shift and drape his arm across Antonio. Most women would be disgusted or bothered by the sight, but I wasn't normal. Something about seeing two men share something physical had always gotten me revved up.

My feet padded across the plush carpet as I made my way to the adjoining bathroom. The face staring back at me was not someone I recognized. The girl in the mirror had been making decisions the Mia I knew wouldn't normally make. As I inspected the glow kissing my skin, I realized the old Mia wasn't who I wanted to be anymore.

After splashing water on my face, I ran my finger over my teeth using some toothpaste I found in the drawer. The cool mint flavor was a small comfort, grounding me as I tried to make sense of my tangled emotions. I looked at my reflection, the lingering heat from last night still visible in the flush of my cheeks and the spark in my eyes.

"I have extra toothbrushes, you know?" Michael stood in the doorway, watching me with a soft smile.

I smiled back as I wiped my hands off on a nearby towel. "I didn't want to wake you."

"How are you feeling? Any regrets?"

Did I have any regrets? I searched my mind for a feeling of guilt but found nothing. "Nope. You?"

"The only regret I have is the timing. Last night was more than I could have ever dreamed of, but the fact is we have a major problem on our hands."

In the distance, I heard the familiar sound of my ringtone going off. "I should answer that."

Michael stepped to the side and handed me one of his T-shirts. "You might want to put this on." He grinned as he ran his hand down my bare skin. "Even if you look good this way."

"Thanks." The shirt hung to my knees, covering my bare bottom as I headed out of his room in search of my phone. As soon as I stepped into the guest bedroom, I grabbed the device off the nightstand. There'd been fifteen missed calls in the last hour from my boss and an additional dozen from Agent Jackson.

Michael furrowed his brows at me. "You look serious."

I glanced at the screen, the multitude of missed calls and messages confirming the urgency. "It's my boss and Agent Jackson. They've been calling non-stop."

Michael's expression turned grave. "What do they want?"

"I don't know, but it can't be good." I swiped to unlock the phone and dialed my boss's number, my heart pounding as I waited for the call to connect. Michael watched me intently, his concern mirrored in the lines of his face.

The phone barely rang once before my boss's voice boomed through the speaker. "Mia, where the hell have you been? We have a situation." His voice faltered, making me tense with concern.

"What? Are you okay, Mike?"

"Turn on your TV, Mia. I thought you were dead. Where are you?"

"Before you freak out, let me explain. I'm at Michael Brighton's house."

"Good," he cut me off.

"Wait. You're not mad that I'm at the defendant's attorney's house?"

"He might be the only one who can protect you. We now know Dmitri Ivanov is targeting us. My family has already been moved to a safe house, and Agent Jackson is here with me now. Mia," he sighed. "I think you're right. Riley Lawson is innocent, and we need to figure out how to clear her name."

"What makes you think Dmitri is targeting us?"

"We are pretty sure he blew up your house."

I stumbled into Michael, who tugged me into his arms and held me steady.

"Let me talk to Brighton."

"He's here. You're on speaker," I whispered, still in shock at the news my house was gone.

"Brighton, how much did you hear?"

"All of it, sir. What can I do to help?"

Antonio walked in, tugging a shirt over his head. "Everything okay?"

"Who else is there?" Mike's voice was tense.

"Um." I paused and took a breath. "Antonio Anastasi."

"Antonio Anastasi?" The surprise in Mike's voice was palpable.

Silence filled the room as the three of us stared at the phone. I had no idea what was running through his mind right now, and honestly, I didn't care. At this point, my job was already tanked. He probably thought I was sleeping with Antonio, which I was, but what he didn't know was I had slept with them both. My body blushed with the memory of our night together.

Mike surprised me when he spoke. "Antonio, can you keep her safe?"

"I can," Antonio replied firmly, his voice steady.

"Do it. I don't care where you take her, just keep her safe. And Antonio…" Mike sighed into the phone. "No one can know she's with you. It would completely unravel your sister-in-law's case. You understand, right?"

"Yes, Sir. I won't tell anyone. Only you and Michael will know."

"We need to keep Dmitri and the FBI in the dark about our newly formed relationship as well. We might be able to use it to our advantage, okay?"

Antonio glanced over at me and smiled. "I understand."

"I'll be in touch." I disconnected the call and tossed my phone onto the bed.

"This is ridiculous. Did you hear what he said? I need to see." I tugged out of Michael's hold and pushed past Antonio to head downstairs.

I had to see for myself. Someone had destroyed my house. The remote felt heavy in my hand as I turned it on to a local station. Sure enough, crews were outside my home, covering the burning mess that had once been my place of residence. Black smoke and charred wood stood frozen on the screen, mocking me from behind the glass. The anchor's voice echoed through the room, his words heavy with fear and sadness.

"Police say the explosion appears to be the work of an arsonist and that they have yet to recover the homeowner— who has now been identified as state prosecutor Mia Hill."

Antonio turned off the TV and stood in front of the screen, blocking my view.

"Mia?" He glanced at Michael and shared a silent understanding. "I know this is hard, but right now, everyone thinks you're dead or missing. We need to let them keep thinking that."

My body dropped without thought to the couch. Overcome with sadness, tears spilled down my cheeks as I stared blankly at the ceiling. "I've ruined everything."

"No." Michael dropped beside me and tugged my hand into his. "You haven't. This is all Dmitri. You aren't the only one whose life he's ruined. You have to know that deep down."

My head knew his words were true, but my heart was fracturing into a thousand pieces—much like the career I had spent the last decade cultivating. I inhaled a deep breath, letting the air fill my lungs, then blew it out. Something needed to change, something drastic.

Was this meant to make me pause and reflect on my life?

It didn't matter. Either way, I was going to have to choose at some point. For now, I just needed to survive.

"What are we going to do now?" I glanced over at Michael, surprised to see the worry etched on his face.

"You'll stay here." He stood and walked over to Antonio. "The longer they think she's dead, the better off she will be."

Antonio nodded and pulled his phone from his pocket as he stepped into the kitchen.

"What about you? Aren't I putting you in danger if I stay here?" I watched Antonio in the kitchen, curious who he called.

"No. This is the safest place for you right now."

"We have a problem." Antonio stepped back into the room, his body tense with emotion. "A shipment has gone missing." His eyes shifted between me and Michael.

"What shipment?" I asked, confusion seeping into my bones.

"Mia. There are things I can't tell you until I know where you stand. For now, you're just going to have to trust I won't do anything that will put you in danger... more danger than you're already in."

"No." I folded my arms across my chest. "Secrets won't work with me. I already have a madman blowing things up after me. I won't have you lying to me, Antonio. I know your family is in the mafia... hell, that's why the feds are so hell-bent on making an example out of Riley, but that's a moot point right now. I've already crossed a line I can't undo."

Michael sighed. "She's right. I think she deserves to know what she's getting into if this is going to become more."

Antonio ran his hand down the stubble forming on his face. "We are in arms dealing, and a shipment of guns has gone missing. Massimo thinks Dmitri is behind it and is planning on using it to frame us somehow. This has become bigger than we expected. Dmitri is hellbent on ruining our family, and he doesn't care who he takes out in the process."

I absorbed his words, rolling them around in my head. I absorbed his words, rolling them around in my head. A part of me knew the Anastasis were into illegal dealings, but until this moment, there had been no actual proof. Now it was out there in the open, and I couldn't live in denial. Was I willing to compromise my belief and give this man a chance? He stood for everything I fought against, yet when I looked at him, my heart hummed so loudly, nothing else seemed to matter.

"Okay," I whispered as I stepped toward him. "I'll stay here."

Antonio blinked, shocked at my reaction. Honestly, I was shocked at my reaction too. I thought there would have been more of an internal battle about what I was getting into, but there wasn't.

"Good. I'm going to grab a few things from my house. Anything you need, we can get for you."

Exhaling, I nodded and headed upstairs to my room.

Never in a million years would I have guessed I would throw away my career for a man. Or that I would be in hiding with the man whose family was at the center of all my problems— but reality was about to set in, and I prayed I wouldn't fall apart.

eleven

MICHAEL

THE ROOM FELT heavy as I stood staring down at Vincenzo Anastasi. He'd always been the tough one in the family, and seeing him fragile, near death like he was now, rattled me beyond comprehension.

"Michael." Massimo stepped into the room with Madison trailing close behind him. "Where's Antonio?"

"He's tied up handling the matter with Mia. How is he?" I cocked my head toward Vincenzo's still form.

"Stable, but not waking up. The doctors aren't sure why, but he's in a coma. Possibly from the blood loss." Massimo ran his hands through his hair, worry etched his features, making him look older than he was. Madison clung to him, her face streaked with the signs of her recent tears, her grip tight and trembling. "Where's Riley?" I glanced around the hospital room, surprised she wasn't present.

"The doctors are checking her over." Madison leaned into her husband, her eyes laden with worry. "She had a fainting spell last night."

"Shit…the babies?"

"They're fine." Riley's voice filled the room. "It's good to see you, Michael." She saddled up next to the bed and tugged Vincenzo's hand into hers. The pain she carried radiated off her in tsunami-sized waves.

My heart clenched seeing her so lost and broken.

"I have some news." All eyes turned toward me, pinning me frozen.

"Well?" Massimo stepped forward, breaking the awkward silence filling the room. He rested his hand on Riley's shoulder, giving her a silent show of support.

"The D.A. and Agent Jackson are working with us to clear Riley's name."

"Why now?" Riley sighed, shaking her head. "Is it because they think Vin is going to—" Her voice cracked. "die?"

"No. The prosecutor, Mia Hill, outed Dmitri to her boss. He went on TV and linked him to Vincenzo's stabbing and your arrest."

"What does that have to do with me?"

"Well…" I swallowed. I had to be careful what I told them. We still didn't know who was listening. "He blew up the prosecutor's house. She's missing."

"Fuck." Massimo ground his teeth together in frustration.

"What about Antonio? Wasn't he working at her place?" Madison's concern showed on her face. She and Antonio were close and knowing he might be hurt or in trouble bothered her.

"Yes, but there is no way they can link him to the explosion. Plus—" I blew out a breath, "Agent Jackson found Dmitri's calling card at the scene."

"He's behind both missing shipments." It wasn't a question. We all suspected it was him, but with everything that happened recently, it was more like an unconfirmed truth. "I need to call Antonio. He doesn't need to stress about this. He's still getting over Grandfather's death and now Vincenzo."

"I'll talk to him." Everyone turned to look at me.

Madison cracked a knowing smile as Massimo cocked an eyebrow in question. "Why would you talk to him?"

"Um." I hesitated, unsure of what to say. I knew Antonio wasn't one hundred percent sure about telling them about us right now, but I hated lying to Massimo.

Madison gave me a knowing glance and tugged on Massimo's arm. "Come on, Massimo. Let's give them some space. They need to figure things out."

Massimo's eyes narrowed in suspicion, but he nodded. "I don't know what you're keeping from me," he glanced between me and Madison, suspicion marring his face, "but I am going to assume whatever it is, it's protecting this family. If I find out otherwise, I won't hesitate to kill you."

"Massimo." Madison slapped his chest. "That is so far out of line. Michael, please forgive his crass remark."

"Massimo, don't scare off my attorney. I need him to get me out of this charge, so my babies aren't being raised by someone else. If Vincenzo dies…" Riley's voice caught with emotion.

"Stop." I pressed my hand to her back. "He isn't going to die. He's too fucking mean. And I didn't take Massimo's statement personally. He's right. I am keeping something from him. But—" I turned to look at him. "It's not what you think. When the time is right, Antonio will tell you himself. Just know I will protect him and your family as if it was my own."

Massimo nodded his head in acceptance. "Fine."

I bid them farewell and headed out of the room. Something had to give, or this would not end the way we needed. I slipped my phone out of my pocket and called the only person who could help me.

"Agent Jackson." I stepped into the elevator, praying my call wouldn't drop. "We need to meet and come up with a plan. This family deserves some peace."

Pulling into the diner's parking lot, I glanced around for any threats looming. The last thing I needed was to have something go wrong now. Agent Jackson was seated at a corner booth, looking as worn as I felt.

"Jackson." I slid into the seat opposite him. "I hope we can work this out together and bring in the man responsible for it all."

"Dmitri Ivanov." He sighed. "That man has been a thorn in the FBI's side for a decade or more. Every time we get close, he somehow evades us. I'll do what I can on my end to redirect the spotlight from your clients if you help me shine it on him."

"That's why I'm here." I smiled, tapping the counter with my knuckles. "Look, there are things you need to know, but I need reassurance you aren't going to use it against Riley or Vincenzo."

Jackson settled against the back of his seat and tugged out his cell phone. He slid it across the surface toward me.

"Take the battery out." I watched as he stood, tore off his jacket and lifted his shirt. "No wire. If you want to pat down my pants, I'm fine with that. I don't give a shit about the Anastasis. Dmitri Ivanov killed my partner's mother."

My shocked expression must have been easily read on my face.

"Yeah. I know about that, Michael. FBI, remember? It wasn't an important detail to mention to anyone, so I didn't. By the time I learned the truth, Riley had already bonded out of jail." He sat back down and sighed. "What I want is Ivanov's head on a platter and my partner to live her life without worrying she's going to give birth in jail."

"You sure you're in the right profession?" I laughed. "Agents aren't usually this forgiving."

He grew silent. His gaze never wavered from mine.

"See… the thing is, Michael. This job took something from me I'll never get back, so everything I do now is for me."

My brows knitted together in confusion. He lifted the glass of water the waitress had placed in front of him and took a sip. I watched with confusion as he set the empty tumbler down and let his arms fall to his sides.

"Jackson… what did the FBI take from you?"

"The woman I loved."

I stared at him, taken aback by the raw emotion in his voice. "What happened?"

He sighed, leaning back in the booth. "We were engaged. She was everything to me. There was a case, one that went south in a way no one saw coming. She got caught in the crossfire, a casualty of a job that was supposed to protect people. The Bureau's response was to cover it up, make it disappear like she never existed. I was supposed to move on, act like it didn't happen."

"Jackson, I'm so sorry. I had no idea."

He waved off my sympathy, his eyes hardening. "That's why this is personal for me. Dmitri Ivanov was behind that operation. He orchestrated the whole thing, and she paid the price. I've been waiting for a chance to take him down ever since."

"Then we have the same goal," I said, determination settling in my chest. "I'll help you get him, and in return, you make sure Riley and Vincenzo are cleared."

Jackson nodded, a flicker of hope in his eyes. "Agreed. But we need to be smart about this. Dmitri has connections everywhere. We can't afford to make a single mistake."

"We won't," I assured him. "I'll talk to Antonio and Mia. We'll coordinate our efforts and make sure we're all on the same page."

"Good." Jackson leaned forward, his voice low and urgent. "Let's start by figuring out Dmitri's next move. He's already targeted you and your people. He'll come after you again, and we need to be ready."

I nodded, feeling the weight of our mission settle heavily on my shoulders. But for the first time, I felt a sense of purpose and clarity. We had a chance to bring Dmitri Ivanov to justice, and I wasn't going to let it slip away.

"I'll be in touch," I said, standing up from the booth. "We'll get through this, Jackson. Together."

He gave me a grim smile. "I hope you're right, Michael. For all our sakes."

Leaving the diner, I felt a renewed sense of determination. I dialed Antonio's number, my mind racing with plans and strategies. We were up against a formidable enemy, but we had something Dmitri didn't: a united front and a personal vendetta that fueled our *every* move.

twelve

ANTONIO

MIA WAS BEAUTIFULLY WRAPPED around Michael. After the first week of being holed up at Michael's house, she'd moved her things into his room. She said she hated being alone in her room at night. I didn't mind—hell, I had practically moved into his place as well. I still hadn't told Massimo what was happening between us, though I suspected he knew.

On the other hand, Madison knew. The day she brought clothes over from Mia, she hugged me and told me it would all work out. She was glad to see me happy. The fact I was in love with Michael and falling hard for Mia didn't faze her. Madison insisted Massimo wouldn't care, either, but I didn't want to add to his stress.

Vincenzo was still in a coma, and Riley was now on bed rest at his side. She'd fought tooth and nail to be in his room. Massimo and my father raised hell with hospital administration to get them to allow it—that and the sizable donation our family made to the hospital.

"Are you just going to stare at us or are you going to get back in bed?" Michael's deep voice gave me goosebumps as I stalked toward the two of them, stripping off my clothes.

I slipped back under the covers and snuggled against Mia's warm body as she pressed her backside into me and giggled. "I think someone is awake."

Michael reached across her body and wrapped his fingers around my rigid shaft. "I'd say so." He smirked as he pumped his fist along my shaft, drawing a groan from between my lips.

My head dipped and sucked Mia's flesh into my mouth as Michael's finger tightened around my cock. Mia spread her legs, silently begging to be filled. Michael wasted no time shifting forward and burying his cock between her dripping wet folds.

"Oh God," she moaned as he backside pressed into my body...

I reached around and cupped her breast. My fingers plucked at her pert nipple, sending shudders through her body. "I want you to lose yourself as he fucks you," I whispered into her ear, sucking her lobe between my teeth, and biting down.

Mia wrapped her arm around my neck and pulled my mouth to hers. Our lips met in burning passion as Michael pumped into her. I held his gaze as my tongue slipped between Mia's lips. My cock grew harder in his hand when he tightened his grip around the sensitive flesh and jerked me in rhythm with their body's movements.

"I wanna fuck him while he's buried inside you." I need to be inside Michael as he drove into Mia was overwhelming, but I needed her to say it was ok. We were still navigating this unorthodox relationship, and with everything else going on around us, I wanted to tread carefully.

Her groan of approval had my dick pulsing with want. When she nodded her head and whispered her approval, Michael rolled her onto her back and tugged her to the edge of the bed. He wedged a pillow beneath her hips, angling himself against her opening and slowly pushed back into her channel.

"Oh God." Mia squeezed her eyes shut as Michael's girth filled her completely. "I feel so full when you're inside me."

Working hard to rein in my exuberance, I grabbed the lube and a condom from the side table before positioning myself behind Michael. The three of us had explored each other quite a bit since she'd come to be here, but this would be the first time I'd taken Michael while he was buried balls deep inside her.

My palms pressed against the globes of his ass. The muscles in his back and thighs flexed with each thrust of his hips into Mia. He hissed as the cool gel dripped down the crack of his ass, coating his hole and readying him to take me. After slipping on a condom, I pressed my lips to his back and pushed the head of my cock between his cheeks. I couldn't take my eyes off Mia. Her gaze was hooded and full of fire as she watched me seat myself fully inside him.

He stilled inside Mia, reveling in the feeling of me buried inside him. I froze behind him, lost to the sensation of his ass clenching around my shaft. Every time he thrusted inside her my cock bobbed inside him. Michael was essentially fucking both of us at one time, and I thought I'd pass out from the extreme pleasure it was bringing me.

Mia cried out, her body racing toward the finish line. Michael sensed her impending orgasm and picked up his speed. Pressing down on his spine, I shifted my body, striking his prostate with each thrust. As the head of my dick brushed the erogenous zone inside him, my body shattered. I cried out, my fingers digging into his flesh as I spilled myself inside him. Michael groaned, his own cock exploding and coating the inside of Mia's womb. He pumped a few more times into her channel before collapsing on top of her. My cock pulled free, cum seeping out of the barrier as I leaned back on my heels.

"Holy shit." He huffed, nearly out of breath as he glanced over his shoulder at me. "That was…"

"Amazing," Mia whispered beneath him. "Next time, I want Antonio to fuck me and you to be on top."

"I think we've created a monster," I laughed as I forced myself to step away and retrieve a towel. After wiping myself off, then cleaning Michael's backside, I turned toward the bathroom. "I'm going to take a shower. We're supposed to meet with Agent Jackson in an hour."

"All right…" Mia groaned and wrapped her arms around Michael as I disappeared into the bathroom. "I guess we can't stay in bed forever."

I wanted to go see Vincenzo today, but first, we had to meet with Agent Jackson. Hopefully, he had some news that would prove this wasn't for nothing.

"Can we join you?" The timbre of Michael's voice drew a smile on my face. I smiled as Michael and Mia sauntered into the bathroom.

"I guess it's a good thing you put a big shower in here."

Thoughts of my brother vanished from my mind as the three of us explored one another beneath the heat of the shower. If this was how it was going to be having them in my life, then I couldn't wait for the future we were building—at least I hoped we were building one. We hadn't discussed where this thing between us was going, but I prayed like hell it was going somewhere permanent.

Once we climbed from the confines of the enclosure, I pulled Mia against my chest and burrowed my face into her wet hair.

"You okay?" Her palm cupped my head against her skin, holding me in place.

"Yeah. Where is this going with us, Mia?" I couldn't stop thinking about what this thing between us meant. Was it just sex for her? Or was she falling for us like I knew we were falling for her?

She turned in my arms and held my cheeks in her hands. "What's this about, Antonio?"

"I don't know," I sighed, pulling free of her grasp. "I'm scared, I think." I turned from her, wiping the remnants of water from my skin. Michael leaned against the doorframe, watching me with compassion. "I've spent my whole life running from things that are hard—specifically love. Accepting who I am lifted a burden off my shoulders, but I'm terrified it's going to crash and burn."

Michael stepped forward, his fingers threading into my hair. He tightened his grip, pulling my head so our gazes collided. "I love you, Antonio. I think I've loved you for months. Nothing about how I feel about you is going to *crash*. Burn? Absofukc-inglutely. *Everything* about you makes me burn with a fire I never thought could exist. You're everything to me and nothing or nobody will *ever* come between us." His lips crashed against mine, rendering me completely speechless. When he finally pulled away, he ran his thumb across my lower lip. The unwavering love that showed in his eyes made my heart beat a little faster. "Stop doubting you deserve this and just love me back." He touched his forehead to mine and sighed.

The sound of Mia's breath hitching had us turning toward her. Her eyes were wet with tears, but the unmistakable look of love shined like the morning sun. Michael dropped his hold on me and took a step back.

"Mia." His voice wavered with emotion as he inched toward her. "This doesn't change how I feel about you."

She glanced toward me, her smile drawing me in her direction like a magnet. "I know." Her eyes cast downward for a minute, making the two of us pause.

Michael and I shared a glance of uncertainty—both of us feeling the same momentary panic that this was too much for her.

We were on her with a quickness she wasn't expecting.

"Mia." My tone was filled with longing. "My heart isn't complete without you. Michael's heart isn't complete without you. We need you. We love you… can't you see that?"

She crashed her lips against mine, her fingers pulling at my flesh to draw me closer.

"Mia." Michael wrapped her in his arms, pulling her between

us as I continued to ravage her lips. "Antonio and I want you as much as we want each other."

She turned her head, breaking our kiss to cover his mouth with hers. When they finally parted, she was panting.

"I…" She pressed her head to mine. "I'm terrified this is going to end."

"Baby, you don't have to say it back to us. When you're ready—and you see, this isn't going to end because I won't let it—you'll know it's the right time." I pressed a kiss to the corner of her mouth. "And as much as I want to bury my cock inside you right now, Agent Jackson is waiting for us." My dick pressed into her belly, making her eyes dilate.

"I think you can be late." She dropped to her knees between us and pulled me into her mouth. Her hand reached back, and she fisted Michael in her palm.

"Holy shit, baby." Michael stumbled forward, not expecting it and nearly knocked us down.

"Jesus Christ." My eyes rolled back into my head as she worked my shaft. The fucking sounds coming out of her mouth had me erupting so fast, the force of my cum hitting the back of her throat made me sag to my knees.

She gave me a devilish smile before turning to Michael's swollen member, which was glistening with precum. Inching closer, I watched with rapt attention as she sent Michael careening over the edge. He scooped her off the ground, pulling her from his flaccid cock, and smashed his lips to hers. Extending his hand, I pressed my palm to his and let him pull me from the ground.

"I'm not sure I know my name." I shook my head as I crushed myself against her backside. "We are two of the luckiest bastards to have found you, Miss Hill."

We finally extracted ourselves from her body and got dressed. Leaving her alone in the house was harder than I imagined, but this meeting would hopefully give us the information needed to end this shit with Ivanov.

Michael and I shared a glance, silently affirming our shared determination as we headed out. The drive to the meeting spot was filled with tension and unspoken thoughts. As we parked and made our way inside, I could feel the weight of our mission pressing heavily on us.

Agent Jackson was already seated, his expression as serious as ever. "You're late," he said, not unkindly, but with a hint of impatience.

"Sorry," Michael replied, taking a seat. "We had to take care of a few things."

Jackson nodded, understanding. "All right, let's get to it. We need to be on the same page if we're going to take down Dmitri."

We leaned in, ready to tackle whatever lay ahead. The stakes were high, but our resolve was unbreakable. With Mia in our hearts and our mission clear, we were ready to face whatever came next.

Or so we hoped.

thirteen

MIA

WHEN THEY LEFT me to meet with Jackson, I'd promised not to leave the house—and until this moment, I'd done just that. But after our heartfelt moment in the shower, my feelings got the better of me. I knew they were doing it to protect me, but being left out sucked.

So, what did I do? I called a cab. After I disarmed the security system, ensuring my ability to get out would go unnoticed, I sauntered down the long driveway and waited for my ride to arrive. Turning off the system was risky, but I knew it would trip an alert to Michael's phone if I didn't.

The driver looked at me like I was crazy when I slipped into the backseat. Fortunately, he didn't say much and kept his eyes on the road. That should have been my first clue that something was wrong. My brain seemed to catch up with the fact we weren't heading in the direction I'd given the driver.

"Excuse me." I leaned forward, trying to get his attention. "You're going the wrong way."

He glanced into the rearview mirror and swallowed. On further inspection, I realized he was covered in a sheen of sweat and acting all kinds of shifty.

"Did you hear me? You're not driving toward town." He continued to ignore me. His knuckles were white as they held onto the steering wheel in a vise grip. "Hey, quit fucking ignoring me." I slapped the back of his seat, but when he still refused to answer me, I screamed at him. "Stop this car right now." My fingers wrapped around the door handle as I shifted closer to the passenger side. "I will fucking jump from this car if you don't stop this instant."

He looked up and sighed. I could see the turmoil in his expression as he squeezed his eyes closed briefly.

"Look, lady, I don't know what you've gotten yourself into, but if I don't take you where I'm supposed to—he'll kill me."

"Who will kill you?" I started jerking on the handle, panic setting in when it didn't give. "Do you know who I am? I'm the fucking state prosecutor… you hear me? If you do this, you'll seal your fate and spend the rest of your life in prison for kidnapping."

"Fuck." His hands tightened around the leather. "This is messed up. You know that, right? I'm just a fucking cab driver."

"Slow down a little, and I'll jump. You can tell whoever threatened you I escaped from the moving car, okay? Just don't take me wherever there is."

He mulled over my words for a moment before easing the car to the edge of the road. Fortunately, we were on a two-lane road shrouded in trees. If I had to guess, we weren't anywhere near Michael's. I'd been so trapped in my head going over their meeting with Agent Jackson, I hadn't paid any attention to the drive… until right then.

"I don't want to die, but I can't in good conscience do this," he whispered, refusing to make eye contact with me. "I'm not a murderer."

"Look, go to the Velvet Ace Lounge and Casino, and find Massimo Anastasi. Tell him Mia Hill sent you. He'll protect you—I swear it." When I heard the lock disengage, I tugged the smooth silver handle, shoved the door open, and jumped out.

Inhaling a deep breath, I rolled away from the car, skidding down the small embankment. Gravel dug into my skin, tearing into the cotton fabric of my leggings.

For what felt like an eternity, I stared at the sky, willing myself to take a breath. Pain radiated through my body in ways I had never experienced. While I didn't think anything was broken, I hurt like hell.

Once I caught my breath enough, I rolled to my knees and pushed to stand. The world tilted on its axis for a moment, causing black dots to swim in my vision. Passing out was the last thing I needed. There was a good chance someone was following him, and I had to get the hell away from here before Dmitri Ivanov came for me. I knew, without a doubt, he was behind this. I'd been so stupid to leave the house.

I was literally in the middle of the desert. Forcing one foot in front of the other, I disappeared into the sparse cover of trees. The brush would give me some cover in the event someone drove down the road. While traipsing through the heat wasn't the brightest idea, taking a chance on a passing car was far more dangerous. Glancing into the sun, I sighed. At least it would be hours before it got dark. Moving farther into the desert, I prayed I was walking in the right direction. Otherwise, Dmitri Ivanov would be the least of my worries come nightfall.

The heat bore down on me even after the sun had set. I had to keep moving despite the fact my feet were killing me. Pain radiated like tiny waves rolling across my body as I forced myself through the sand. I didn't know where I was or if I was even going in the right direction.

One thing was certain. Ivanov and his goons wouldn't find me—but neither would anyone else. After wandering through a few cacti, I finally accepted I had no sense of direction and was lost. The sun, now hidden beneath the earth, only succeeded in making the desert dark and creepy. Putting the sounds of wildlife out of my mind was not an easy feat.

Eventually, I'd find a road—or more desert. My foot caught a downed tree, causing me to pitch forward and land on my hands and knees. More pain lanced through my body, my spine protesting at the blunt force. A part of me wanted to lie down and just give up. This is what I deserved for leaving Michael's house. After taking a few deep breaths, I forced myself to stand. My eyes clenched shut in response to the burning sensation traveling through my veins. Ivanov might not have killed me, but this fucking wasteland probably would.

When I finally opened my eyes, I was certain I was hallucinating. The bright lights of the downtown Vegas strip loomed in the distance. I wanted to run toward the neon savior that was beckoning me forward, but I was scared. If Ivanov's men were somewhere out there, I was as good as dead, but I had to find help. Refusing to give him what he wanted, I slowly pushed through the bushes, hiding among the shadows of the buildings.

People shot me a few puzzled expressions but made no attempt to help or stop me. I was pretty sure I looked like a homeless person, or worse, a crackhead, but that allowed me to move through the city without being bothered. Vincenzo's restaurant was closest, but the people there didn't know me. There was only one option—the Velvet Ace Lounge and Casino. I knew Antonio's brother, Massimo, lived on the top floor, so my chances of finding someone who could help there were significantly higher.

I hugged the brick walls as I edged my way down the strip, ducking my head when anyone looked at me. The bright sign of the Velvet Ace Lounge and Casino gleamed against the night sky like a beacon of hope, calling me forward. A massive line of people wrapped around the sidewalk, waiting to get in. I didn't look like someone who belonged in the club because my clothes were ripped, and my body was littered with bruises and scrapes. Not to mention, I felt as bad as I looked and was near to passing out from exhaustion and dehydration. Turning on my heel, I found myself in the alley. It was dimly lit, casting an eerie glow across the pave-ment. Of course, the back door was locked. My eyes welled with tears as I slid down the hard surface of the wall. My energy was gone, and I couldn't force myself to go back out front.

"Hey, are you all right?"

A woman's voice startled me, causing my eyes to snap open. My vision swam, blurring as I tried to see who was standing in front of me.

"Holy shit. Freddy, get Massimo. It's Mia." A warm hand pressed down on my shoulder. "Mia? Honey, can you hear me?"

I blinked, unable to speak. The wear and tear on my body finally made it impossible. Exhaustion demanded I close my eyes and give in to the darkness dancing through my mind.

"I got her, Madison." Strong arms lifted me from the ground, cradling my body as I was carried inside.

The rhythmic motion of his movements told me we were still walking. Familiar sounds of an elevator opening filtered through my ears.

"How did she get out there?"

"I don't know, Massimo. She didn't say anything."

"Call Antonio. He needs to know she's here. I'm calling Catarina. She needs to be looked over. I'm concerned she needs a hospital."

Massimo, who I assumed had been carrying me, laid me down on something soft. I tried to open my eyelids, but they felt like they'd been glued shut. No longer able to fight the pull of darkness, I let myself succumb.

For the first time, in what had to have been hours, I was finally safe.

ANTONIO

"ANTONIO," Massimo growled through the phone, his irritation clear in his tone.

"What's the matter?" I glanced over at Michael, who was driving us home from our meeting with Agent Jackson. "Is it Vin?"

"No, he's fine. There's a man at the club who says he was told to find me for protection, but he won't say anything more to Donny. I'm headed there now."

"Who would tell him to come to you for protection? And protection from what?"

"That's the thing." Massimo sighed, a rare sound from my hardened brother. "He said Mia Hill sent him."

I tensed my grip tightening on the phone. "Mia? That makes no sense."

"No shit. That's why I'm calling you. What the fuck aren't you telling me, Little Brother?"

I hesitated, knowing I needed to tell him Mia had been staying with us. Massimo was sharp, he'd read between the lines. This was more than protecting the woman responsible for clearing Riley's name or ruining it.

"Mia isn't missing. She's been staying at Michael's house."

"Come again?" Massimo snapped, his voice rising several octaves.

"Look. Agent Jackson and the D.A. know Riley is innocent. When they outed Ivanov on the news, Dmitri blew up Mia's house. She went to Michael's house, and we've been protecting her ever since. I wanted to tell you, but Agent Jackson and the D.A. felt the fewer people who knew she wasn't dead, the better."

"I see." He got quiet, the silence heavy and unnerving. "Can you ask her why she sent someone to my club for protection? We'll deal with the other matter later."

"We aren't with her. Michael and I met with Agent Jackson about the case. She's back at Michael's house."

Keeping my brother on the line, I watched as Michael pressed the call button and dialed Mia. The ringing filled the car's interior, each unanswered ring stretching my nerves taut. When her voicemail picked up, he tried again.

"Fuck, she's not answering."

"I'll call you from the club. I'm almost there."

I tossed my phone to the dashboard and turned to Michael. He was still calling her phone, only to have her voicemail pick up each time.

"What the fuck?" Michael grunted. "If someone came on the property, I would know. Nothing's gone off. Maybe she's in the bathtub."

"Right… a bath. After that long shower we took?" I bit back, my words sharp with unintentional cruelty. I wanted him to be right, but my gut told me something was seriously wrong. "I will kill Dmitri if she's hurt, Michael. That man has tried to take everything from my family."

Michael laced his fingers with mine and squeezed. "I know." What more could he say?

He was just as worried about Mia as I was, but he was trying to keep it together for me as usual. Michael eased down his long drive and slowed the car to a stop. I hopped out, rushing up the steps and inside. The house was just as we had left it, and there were no signs of trouble.

"Mia?" I called out, my voice echoing through the empty rooms as I moved through the lower level, checking for her. My feet skipped steps as I ran upstairs in search of her. "Rach? She's not up here, Michael."

"Antonio." Michael's tone sent a chill through my veins.

I practically jumped down the flight of steps and raced into the living room. Michael was holding her phone in his hand.

"This was on the table." He pinned me with a stare that curdled my blood. "She left us. Mia… she's gone."

"What do you mean, Michael?" I refused to believe she just leave. "She wouldn't just leave us."

"She called a cab." He turned the phone toward me, showing the website of a local company.

My phone rang, interrupting us.

"What?" I snapped into the speaker.

"Brother," Massimo spoke softly, his voice holding a hint of sadness. "Mia's in trouble."

"Fuck. Let me guess. The man was her cab driver."

"Yep. Ivanov somehow intercepted her cab request and threatened this driver. He was supposed to bring her to a location and dump her there."

"I'm going to kill him."

"Hold on a second, Antonio. He didn't do it. Mia convinced him to slow the car and let her jump out. He came straight here."

"Where did he take her?"

"South of Michael's somewhere. It's a back road off the main highway—Hickory Ridge. You know it?"

"Yes. We're heading out now to look for her."

Michael watched me with wide eyes as I threw my phone onto the couch.

"Goddamn it!" I screamed out, my hands immediately fisting the short strands of my hair.

"Calm down. We'll find her." Michael tugged me into an embrace. "She's going to be fine. Mia is a strong woman."

"What if Ivanov finds her first?"

Michael pulled his phone out and pressed the speaker button. "Let's make sure that doesn't happen."

Donny's voice filtered into the room. "Michael?"

"Donny, I assumed Massimo told you what's going on."

"I'm still here with him and the driver. I was the one here when he came in talking crazy. Look…" Donny paused. "You and Antonio stay put. My guys are headed that way now and will search for her. If she makes it home, she's going to need you both."

"You expect us to just sit here and wait on her?" I bellowed into the room. My restraint was gone.

Donny grew silent. "I see."

"See what, Donny? Mia is being hunted." I scoffed.

"You're in love with her. What other reason would you have for reacting like this?"

"What?" I growled, trying not to lose my shit more.

"It's no big deal if you are, but this changes things. She's not just someone who can save Riley. She's important to you."

"Jesus Christ, Donny. I didn't realize you were a relationship guru, nor did I realize you were so interested in my love life."

"Get a grip, Antonio. I just thought…" His voice trailed off, causing me to glance at Michael.

"You thought what?"

"I thought you and Michael were a thing." I could hear the grin in his tone, though his answer wasn't what I suspected.

"Fuck." Michael shook his head. "Look, Donny. Now isn't the time to get into this. Can you just focus on finding her? We can worry about this later." Michael slammed the phone down when it went dead, filling the room with a deafening silence.

Somehow, Donny knew about Michael. Which made me wonder if Massimo knew, and just hadn't said anything.

"He knows about us."

"It's not important right now." Michael shoved the phone in his pocket and walked toward the security room. "I don't understand how she got out without tripping the alarm."

I followed him into the tiny room and smiled when I realized how—Mia had disarmed the entire system. I could see the turmoil etched in the lines of Michael's face. He was blaming himself since he'd shown her how to operate it, in the event she needed help. I never thought she would use it to sneak out, though.

"We shouldn't have kept her in the dark." Michael shook his head, regret etched deeply in his features. "If we had been honest about everything we knew, maybe she wouldn't have felt the need to leave."

"Let's go sit down. There's no sense standing around bitching. You're right, Donny will find her… and when he does, I'm going to spank her ass."

"What if he doesn't?" Michael sighed, his shoulders sinking under the weight of his worries.

"I thought I was the worrier?" I cocked an eyebrow at him, attempting to inject some levity into the situation. "She's strong… remember?"

"Yeah, you're right."

Michael and I sat down, the oppressive silence wrapping around us like a shroud. There was nothing we could do but wait. Donny would find her if Mia was still out there. If she wasn't… I would kill Ivanov with my bare hands. It was already dark, and not knowing when she left meant we didn't know how long she'd been gone. Michael and I had been with Agent Jackson for a couple of hours. My gut churned with worry, the anticipation gnawing at me.

My pulse quickened when I saw Madison's name flash across my screen. Michael shared the same concerned expression when I shot him a look and pressed the device to my face.

"Madison?" I held my breath.

"Antonio, you need to come to the club. We have Mia."

"What?" Blood rushed into my ears. "Say that again."

"She's here." My brothers voice held an air of worry that made my skin crawl.

Michael's face filled with concern, his eyes watery with emotions I knew reflected in my own as I held his gaze and asked, "Why didn't you bring her back to Michael's?"

"She walked to the club, Antonio. I found her outside the back entrance, nearly unconscious."

"We'll be there in thirty." I shoved the phone into my pocket and turned to Michael. "Mia showed up at the Velvet Ace Lounge and Casino. Madison found her nearly unconscious in the alley."

"Let's go." He stood and headed toward the door. "I'll drive."

We climbed into the car, silence filling the space like an

unwelcome guest. Michael laced his fingers with mine and finally spoke. "She's going to be fine."

"I know, but being here isn't safe for her. She needs to go where she won't be a target so easily."

His sigh told me he'd been thinking the same thing. "What are you thinking?"

"Italy. No one would dare touch her there. It worked for Madison… it could work for her."

Michael nodded in understanding. He didn't want her in danger any more than I did. Ivanov proved he was watching her, even in a place as secure as Michael's.

He pulled into the alley and parked his car. I keyed in the code, and we let ourselves inside. The steady thump of music filled the hallway as the lights of the club ricocheted off the walls. Carlisle tipped his head as we passed the bar and headed toward Massimo's private elevator. The ride up to his apartment felt like an eternity.

As soon as the doors parted, Madison greeted Michael and me. "Hey." She wrapped her arms around my waist, halting me in place. I hugged her back, my eyes scanning the room for our girl. "She's still asleep. Catarina is on her way to check her out."

I stepped out of her hold and moved to the bed. Mia was unconscious on their bed. Her blonde hair was matted and stained with a layer of dirt. Seeing her flawless skin marked with cuts and bruises, I couldn't stifle my gasp. Her clothes were tattered with rips, barely covering her body. My fury boiled when my eyes landed on her feet. She was missing a shoe, and the bare foot was red and swollen, covered in dried blood.

"Motherfucker." I ran my hand down her arm and whispered her name. "Mia? Honey, can you hear me?"

Nothing. Not even a whimper escaped her lips. I glanced at Michael, who had stepped beside me and rested his palm against my shoulder. He wore the same pained expression as me.

"Where the fuck is Catarina?" I growled in frustration.

"Calm down. She's coming, and for now, Mia's safe." Michael squeezed my hand, lacing our palms together.

"Antonio?" Massimo stood at the foot of the bed with his eyes riveted to our entwined fingers.

I could read the confusion in his gaze. Neither of us had told him about the relationship we were forming with each other —much less the one with Mia. "Massimo, I need to tell you some things, but right now, I need her to be okay." My eyes closed as I drew in a deep breath.

"I hear you, *fratello*. Just answer me this." He glanced at her still form. "Is she more than someone you're just protecting?"

"Is there some reason you keep yanking me from work?" The sound of Catarina's voice filled the room. She stormed in and huffed when she saw Mia. "What the fuck?" She pushed past Michael and shoved at my shoulder. "Move. Jesus Christ… why can't you people do anything like normal folks?"

Stepping back, I watched as my sister tended to the woman I loved. Michael wrapped his arm around my shoulder and stood next to me, his eyes trained on Mia.

"I'm going to take her to Italy," I said, my sight never wavering from her still form.

"That's probably a good idea." Massimo cleared his throat. "Let Catarina work. We need to talk."

Michael guided me to the living room, where we sat down. Massimo seemed intrigued by the tenderness Michael was showing me. Normally, I'd pull away from him, but that was in the past. Right now, I needed him almost as much as he needed me. When my eyes met my brother's gaze, I was shocked to find curiosity there. I'd expected disgust or anger, but his tender expression held neither.

"So." He blew out a breath. "You and the prosecutor." His eyes moved toward the bed briefly before coming back to my own.

"I'm falling in love with her... no, I'm in love with her. It's stupid of me to lie to you about that... but..." I swallowed my nerves down. "There's more." I glanced at Michael, seeking his silent approval. When he nodded and his fingers tightened around mine, I turned back to my brother. "I love Michael as well."

Massimo leaned back in the seat and crossed his leg over his knee. Madison sat down beside him and pressed her hand to his thigh. I felt like we were waiting for a bomb to go off, and the longer it took him to speak, the more nervous I got.

"That makes more sense." Massimo sighed. "Antonio." He draped his arm over Madison's shoulder and toyed with her hair. "I've suspected you were gay for a long time, but I wanted you to tell me, not me confront you. What I wasn't prepared for was the possibility you were bisexual. Regard-less—" he blew out a breath, "I love you. Was this the secret you refused to tell me?" He turned to Michael and pinned him with a glare.

"Yes." He squeezed my hand held in his. "I wanted Antonio to be the one to tell you."

Massimo held his gaze. "And do you love him?"

"I do… and Mia, too. It's still new, but we've all come to the realization life is too short to live by anyone else's standards."

"All right then." Massimo smiled. "This changes things. I'll call the plane. Once Catarina clears her to fly, you and Mia will leave for Italy."

I furrowed my brow, glancing at the first most important person in my life. "What about Michael?"

"I need to stay here." Michael squeezed my hand again. "Riley needs me in case something happens with the trial. The feds have turned their focus to Ivanov, but that doesn't mean they'll forget about her case. They're determined to make an example out of her… out of our family."

My heart swelled hearing him say *our* family.

"He's right, Antonio. He'll be protected—would have been no matter what, but now that he's part of our family, we'll see nothing happens to him. He's not just our attorney anymore," Massimo tried to comfort my worry.

I didn't like it, but he was right. This whole mess was about more than Mia. It was about saving my family—and he was a key part of that happening. I was about to voice my agreement when Catarina's voice cut through the tension.

"Antonio, she's awake."

MIA

THE PAIN WAS EVEN WORSE than I remembered. A relentless mixture of aches and burns blanketed my entire body, each throb and sting competing for dominance. But the pain in my feet topped everything—a searing, pulsating agony that seemed to radiate up through my legs, making it nearly impossible to focus on anything else. It felt like my feet were being slowly torn apart, every nerve ending ablaze.

I tried to move, but even the slightest shift sent waves of fresh pain coursing through me. The sensation was overwhelming, a brutal reminder of my ordeal. My skin felt raw and tender, as if it had been scraped against sandpaper, while my muscles screamed with a deep, bone-weary fatigue. My head throbbed with a dull, persistent ache, and each breath I took was accompanied by a sharp, stabbing pain in my ribs.

I blinked open my eyes, the brightness of the room assaulting my senses. The light was harsh, piercing through the haze of pain and fatigue, making me wince and turn my head away. Everything around me was a blur, a jumble of indistinct shapes and colors. Slowly, my vision began to clear, and I could make out the figure of a woman leaning over me.

She held a tiny pin light, which she shined directly into my pupils. The beam of light felt like a needle stabbing into my brain, and I flinched, trying to pull away. Her face came into focus—stern, concerned, but professional. Her movements were methodical, her expression intense as she assessed my condition.

"Antonio," she called out, her voice cutting through the fog in my mind. "She's awake."

I turned my head, the effort monumental, and searched for him. Antonio's frame filled my vision as he moved closer, his presence a lifeline amid the pain. He sat on the bed, his hand warm and comforting as it pressed gently to my forehead. The familiar touch grounded me, offering a fleeting sense of security amid the chaos.

"Mia." His voice was a raw whisper, thick with emotion, as he leaned down. His breath was warm against my skin, and his face pressed into the curve of my neck. "I thought we lost you."

The intensity of his relief and fear washed over me, and I could feel the tremble in his body as he held me close. His words reverberated through me, pulling me back from the edge of unconsciousness. The familiar scent of him, mixed with the lingering aroma of the desert dust on my skin, made my eyes sting with tears.

"I…" My throat was so dry it felt like sandpaper, and my voice was barely a whisper. I tried to speak, to offer him some comfort, but my body refused to cooperate. When I attempted to sit up, my muscles screamed in protest. Before I could even begin to struggle, Michael was there on the other side, his hand sliding behind my back with a tenderness that made my heart ache.

"Let me help you," he said, his voice cracking with emotion. His eyes, usually so steady and composed, reflected the turmoil inside him. He moved carefully, his hands steady but gentle as he eased me into a sitting position, supporting my weight as if I were made of glass.

"Here." The woman from earlier—Catarina—shoved a glass of water into Michael's hand, her tone brisk but not rude. "See if she can drink this. Aside from some scrapes, she's just dehydrated."

Michael took the glass, his fingers brushing against mine as he guided it to my lips. The coolness of the water was a balm to my parched throat, and I swallowed eagerly, the relief immediate. My hands trembled as I clutched the cup, draining it quickly. When it was empty, I looked up at Catarina. Her face was a mixture of professional detachment and genuine concern.

I wrapped my hand around the cup and swallowed with eagerness. When the glass was completely drained, I glanced at the woman, who was still watching me with concern.

"Can I have more?" I managed to croak out, my voice still weak but stronger than before.

She nodded, her stern expression softening slightly. "I'm Catarina, by the way. That oaf's sister," she said, nodding toward Antonio as she took the glass from me and turned away to refill it. I noticed Massimo and his fiancée Madison watching from their perch on the couch, their eyes filled with worry and relief as they observed the scene.

Antonio's touch was gentle and reassuring as he smoothed his palm down my arm. "Baby," he murmured, his voice a low rumble. "Can you tell us how you got here or why you left the house?"

I took a deep breath, trying to steady myself. "I was so pissed that you two were keeping things from me," I began, my voice still hoarse. "I thought I could find and confront you guys, but Ivanov must have bugged my phone. How else could he have found me? He threatened the cab driver, coercing him into delivering me to him. Oh my God." My eyes widened as the memory flooded back. "Is the driver safe?"

"He's fine. Don't worry about him." Michael rubbed my leg as though he needed the contact to ensure I was real. "What happened when you realized the driver was taking you to him?"

"He didn't want to be involved, but he was scared. I convinced him to let me jump out by promising your protection. I'm sorry, Mr. Anastasi." I caught Massimo's gaze, his eyes focused intently on me.

"Please call me Massimo, Mia. And don't apologize. You did the smart thing sending him here, or we wouldn't have known to look for you."

"I figured he would tell you, then you two would come for me. Only I got lost in the desert. Stupid me thought I knew where I was going." I laughed nervously. The sound brittle in the room. "Obviously, a sense of direction is not something I possess. I wasn't sure how much longer I could walk. My entire body hurt, and I stumbled so many times." My head shook at the memory of wandering around in the dark. "Then

I saw the strip. I knew if I could get to the Velvet Ace Lounge and Casino, I'd find help."

"Madison found you outside the back entrance, barely conscious," Antonio said, his voice filled with a mixture of relief and lingering fear.

"I remember…" I smiled weakly at the beautiful woman leaning against Massimo. "Thank you."

"Of course. You're going to be family, I suspect. Plus, you might be the key to freeing my sister-in-law, Riley."

"I hope so." I took the glass Catarina had refilled and drank eagerly. "What now? Apparently, Ivanov knows I'm alive."

"As soon as Catarina says you can travel, we are getting on a plane to Italy," Antonio said firmly, his eyes never leaving mine.

My pulse quickened as his words registered. "No. I can't leave now. What about the case?"

"It's temporary. We need to put some distance between you and Ivanov. He wouldn't dare mess with you there. Please, Mia, do this for us." Antonio tugged my hand into his, his grip firm yet gentle, and pressed his lips to the tender flesh. The warmth of his kiss sent a shiver through me. I felt a mixture of reassurance and the fear of the unknown.

"You can go now." Catarina's eyes bounced between the three of us. Her confusion was evident. Antonio held my hand with an intensity that spoke volumes, while Michael still had his hand pressed firmly behind my back, supporting me. "You're just scraped up. Once you take a shower, you'll feel tons better."

"Thank you, Catarina, for coming so quickly." Massimo stood and engulfed his sister in a bear hug. He whispered something in her ear, causing her eyes to flick to Antonio. Understanding dawned in her gaze, and her lips curved into a knowing smile. Massimo stepped back and addressed everyone in the room. "I'll ask Donny to take you home. Ivanov is going to hurt us however he can. That includes you."

Catarina bristled at his comment and rolled her eyes. "I don't need a babysitter."

"Donny has been protecting you since this shit started. Get over it, Cat. I need you safe right now, okay?" Massimo's tone softened, but the worry in his eyes remained.

"Fine. I'll see you guys later. Mia, Michael, welcome to the family. Baby brother, we'll talk about this—" she waggled her finger at the three of us, "later. Be safe."

I watched as she walked to the elevator and climbed inside. Something told me she wasn't someone to mess with either. This entire family was powerful—not just the men. The realization hit me that I was surrounded by protectors, people who would go to any length to keep their loved ones safe.

"Take me home so I can get a shower, and we can leave. Michael's coming with us, right?" My gaze flickered between Antonio and Michael, but in my gut, I already knew the answer.

"No, I need to be here for Riley." Michael leaned down and pressed a tender kiss to my cheek, his lips lingering as if to imprint his promise. "Antonio will go with you, and when this mess is over, we will have all the time together we need, okay?"

The idea of leaving Michael behind was almost unbearable. I hated everything about this. Running away from a problem wasn't something I was used to, but I'd put everyone in danger with my impulsive decision to out Dmitri Ivanov. The weight of my choices pressed down on me, making it hard to breathe.

Going to Italy was the only sensible option—even if it meant leaving Michael behind to deal with the shitstorm I had created. The thought of being separated from him made my chest tighten, but I knew it was necessary. I had to trust that this temporary separation would keep us all safe.

Antonio's hand squeezed mine, pulling me from my thoughts. "We'll get through this, Mia. I promise you."

I nodded, swallowing the lump in my throat. "Okay. Let's go home."

The car ride was quiet, filled with the tension of unspoken fears and the weight of the impending separation. Antonio drove with one hand on the wheel and the other holding mine, his thumb stroking soothing circles on my skin. Michael sat in the back, his eyes never leaving me, as if he could will me to stay by sheer force of will.

When we arrived, I headed straight to the shower, desperate to wash away the grime and the remnants of my ordeal. The hot water cascaded over me, soothing my aching muscles, and bringing a semblance of relief. I let the tears fall, mixing with the water as I released the pent-up fear and frustration.

After I was dressed and ready, I found Antonio waiting for me by the door, his face a mask of determination. "Ready?" he asked softly.

I took a deep breath and nodded. "Ready."

Michael walked over and pulled me into a tight embrace, his arms wrapping around me like a protective cocoon. "Stay safe, Mia. I'll be counting the days until we're together again."

"I will," My voice was thick with emotion as I whispered my reply. "I love you, Michael."

"I love you too," His voice cracking as he replied.

Antonio placed a gentle hand on my shoulder, guiding me toward the door. "Let's go."

As we drove away, I looked back at Michael, standing on the porch, watching us leave. The image of him standing there, strong, and resolute, would stay with me until we were reunited. For now, I had to focus on the immediate future and trust that we would come back together when this was all over.

sixteen

MIA

HER EYES never left the tiny square of plexiglass as the plane taxied down the runway and lifted into the air. Every part of her screamed with the tension riddling her body. I couldn't blame her—her entire life had imploded right before her eyes, both literally and figuratively. Mia was everything I should've avoided but couldn't. And now, her life was in danger because of her affiliation with my family. That, and the stupid decision to put a spotlight on Ivanov.

"Mia?" I said her name softly, startling her from her frozen state. "Do you want to talk about it?"

"What's there to talk about?" she replied, her voice tinged with bitterness. She turned her head toward me and forced a smile that didn't reach her eyes. "I didn't think about the fact that outing Dmitri Ivanov would have a price this steep." She shrugged her shoulders, the motion stiff and uneasy. "I was shortsighted, focused on what it could do for my career and Riley's case." Her eyes shimmered with unshed tears. "Another thing I didn't count on was you and Michael."

"What do you mean?" I asked, shifting nervously in the seat, my heart pounding as I waited for her explanation.

"I tried to bury my feelings for Michael by sleeping with someone I thought was just another guy." Her voice was barely above a whisper, filled with regret.

"If you had known who I was, would that have changed things?" I asked, my voice low and uncertain.

She appraised me for a moment, then sighed deeply. "No, I don't think it would have, and that's the part I'm struggling with. I was supposed to be putting someone you care about behind bars, simply because she fell in love with an Anastasi. Yet…" She closed her eyes and leaned her head back against the seat, her voice trembling. "I did the same thing."

"You're falling in love with me isn't a bad thing, is it?" I leaned forward, pressing my hand to her knee, desperate for her to understand.

"No." She jerked upright, her eyes wide with shock. "I… shit." Mia shook her head, frustration clear on her face. "What I meant was I'm tangled up with the Anastasi family, just like she is. It makes me a hypocrite."

"Aren't you trying to prove Riley's innocence? That's why you ousted Ivanov, isn't it? That must count for something. Deep down, you know she's not guilty and you don't want to be the one to ruin a family," I said, my voice gentle, trying to soothe her inner turmoil.

"You're right," she whispered, her eyes filled with a mix of sadness and determination. "I hate everything about this case. Just because the FBI has a hard-on for Vincenzo doesn't make this right. Part of me wishes they would just handle this case and leave me out of it, but I know if that happened, I wouldn't find the truth."

"And what do you think the truth is?" I asked gently, sensing there was more she needed to say.

"Honestly?" She nibbled her bottom lip, her hesitation palpable.

"Yes, honestly."

"I think the man Riley killed was there to kill Vincenzo, but it backfired. And…" Mia took a deep breath, her eyes clouded with uncertainty as she held my stare.

"And, what?"

"Vincenzo killed him, and Riley is covering for him. She knows if the feds thought for a second he was the one who took Donat's life, they'd lock him away, never to see daylight again. Her love for him is too strong to take that risk. So, instead, she took the fall."

I tried to hide the shock at her accurate account of events. "And what would you do if you found that to be the case?"

Mia reached out and laid her hand over mine, her fingers tracing the top of my knuckles. "Not a damn thing. Dmitri Ivanov and his brother are the scum of the earth. Riley or Vincenzo did the world a service by ending that monster's life. I just wish it had been Dmitri Ivanov instead. That's part of the conundrum I am dealing with." She laced her fingers with mine. "I'm the state's prosecutor, and I'm on a plane with a man who is tied to the family we're investigating. After this is over, I'm not sure I can continue being that person anymore."

"You could always work with Michael."

"I don't know if that would be a good idea, either."

"Why not?"

"Because I have feelings for him, too." She grinned, a hint of mischief in her eyes. "It could make work messy."

"Or it could make it wonderful. Stop thinking so much with your head and start listening to your heart." I tugged her hand to my lips and pressed a kiss to her fingers. "Now." I unbuckled and moved to sit beside her. "How are you feeling?"

"Fine." She shifted toward me, leaning into my warmth. "Are your parents okay with me going to Italy?"

"Yes. They know your predicament and won't hold your current position against you unless you give them a reason not to trust you. Plus, with them back in Vegas with Riley, they're happy someone will be at the house with Nonna. They also know to keep our presence in Italy from the others. Mom and Dad know it is paramount no one finds out we are together."

"I hate this." Mia leaned into me. Her voice was filled with a weary resignation. "Tell me about you and Michael?" Her voice was soft, almost hesitant.

"What about us?"

"When did you and he…" Her voice trailed off, unsure of how to phrase her question.

"Become a couple?"

She nodded against my chest. Her breath was warm through my shirt.

"We hadn't really been one until you." I blew out my breath, the confession weighing heavy on my heart. "He and I explored the feelings we have for each other a while back, but I freaked out. My family didn't know until tonight, and I feared their reactions. At first, Michael didn't understand why I wanted to hide things."

"And now?"

"I love him, and he knows that. I want everyone to know that he's a part of me. It was a relief to hear Massimo accepted things with him… and you. I still need to tell Vincenzo, and that scares the shit out of me."

"I don't think it should. Massimo seemed fine about things. But Antonio…I still don't understand how I'll fit into this scenario."

"That's up to you. You know we're both in love with you. We want you to be part of us if that's something you could see happening. What we are asking is unconventional—I get that —but we won't push you, Mia. Michael and I can only hope you'll let us into your heart. I'm in love with you, but I'll always love and need Michael. If that is not something you can deal with, then we'll never be more than we are now, as much as that pains me to say. I've lived my life by everyone else's standards for too long. I'm done pretending I'm someone I'm not."

Mia's eyes glistened with unshed tears as she processed my words. "Antonio, I care about you both deeply. This situation is far from normal, but nothing about our lives is normal, is it?" she paused, seeming to think about her next words. "Is it weird to you that I want the both of you?"

"No, it isn't," I agreed, my voice soft but firm. "But we can make it work if you want it to. If you want us."

She took a deep breath, her grip on my hand tightening. "I do want you both. I'm just scared of what that means for all of us."

"I realize you can love more than one person romantically. Love isn't something you can turn off or control. It's an emotion meant to be shared, and that doesn't always look the same for people. It's meant to be shared with all the important people in your life—family, friends, or *lovers*." I arched my brow at her and smirked. "If you go into a relationship with your eyes wide open, you can have anything you want. For me, that's Michael and you. But if I have to choose, it will always be Michael." As much as it hurt to say, I knew it was the truth. I wouldn't walk away from Michael willingly.

"I wouldn't ask you to make a choice—not when I have feelings for both of you. And the fact that you love him makes me fall a little harder. Did Michael tell you we'd met before all this?" Mia's eyes held a playful glint, mixed with genuine curiosity.

"No." I shook my head and smiled, intrigued. "But there's been a lot going on."

"True. He and I ran into each other at a bar when I first moved to Vegas." Mia's smile widened, her eyes sparkling with the memory. "I was insanely attracted to him but learned who he was from a friend. I was so mean to him, but that didn't stop him."

"Stop him from what?" I asked, leaning in, eager to hear more.

"Kissing me." Mia blushed, a delicate pink tinting her cheeks. "It was in the hallway by the bathrooms. I was so pissed and turned on at the same time." She giggled. It was light and infectious. "After that, I avoided seeing him in person. I knew if I did, I would betray my career and do something about the desire I'd felt that first encounter."

I brushed my thumb across her knuckles, feeling the warmth of her skin. "And it doesn't bother you that he and I are together?"

"As you've witnessed yourself, it's a tremendous turn-on to see you two together." Her eyes darkened, her voice dropping to a husky whisper.

"A turn-on, huh?" I shifted in the seat, my knees pressing against hers, closing the distance between us.

"Yes." Her eyes dilated, reflecting the desire that sparked between us. I could see she was lost in the memory of our night together, and it sent a thrill through me.

"Are you thinking about us together, Mia?" I asked, my voice low and intimate, the tension between us palpable.

She bit her lip, her cheeks flushing deeper. "Mm-hmm," she mumbled, her voice barely audible.

"Is it getting you wet?" I whispered, unbuckling her seatbelt and lifting the armrest that separated our seats.

Mia's breath hitched. Her eyes locked onto mine with an intensity that made my heart race. "Yes," she breathed, her voice trembling with anticipation.

I cupped her breast through the thin T-shirt she wore, causing her to suck in a breath and arch into my hold. She licked her lips and held my gaze as my palm brushed down the front of her belly and found the waistband of her leggings. I watched for signs she was hurting and needed me to stop. Eager for my touch, Mia leaned back against the seat, encouraging me further. I slid closer to her, my hand slipping beneath her skirt, my fingers brushing against the damp fabric of her panties. The heat from her body was intoxicating, and I could feel her shiver under my touch. "You're soaked, Mia," I murmured, my lips grazing her ear.

She moaned softly, her body arching toward mine. "Antonio…" Her voice was a mix of need and longing, and it drove me wild.

I leaned in, capturing her lips in a searing kiss, my hand moving with deliberate slowness as I teased her. She responded eagerly, her hands clutching at my shirt, pulling me closer. The feel of her against me, the taste of her lips, it all made the world outside the plane cabin disappear. I pushed my fingers in and out of her channel. My lips found hers just in time to swallow her screams as the orgasm ripped from her body and her walls clamped down on my digits. Her body pulsed with release, but I needed more. I scooped her off the seat and carried her to the tiny bedroom in the back of the plane, tossing her onto the bed. I scanned her body.

"If you're too sore for this, we can stop."

Mia shook her head as she propped herself up on her elbows, a playful smile curling on her lips as I began to tug off my clothes. Her eyes sparkled with anticipation, and her breath quickened. I watched her, captivated, as my cock sprang free, hard and ready, bouncing against my belly.

Gripping her leggings, I pulled them down, stripping her bare. Mia fumbled with her shirt, her hands trembling slightly as she slipped it over her head and threw it to the floor. Her skin glowed in the dim light, every curve and line drawing me closer.

We didn't need words. Our bodies communicated with an intimacy that transcended language. As I slid into her warmth, a gasp escaped her lips, and she wrapped her legs around my waist, pulling me deeper. Every stroke of my hips seemed to edge us both closer to the promised land. Her slick, pulsing warmth wrapped around me like a blanket of pure heaven.

Our moans filled the tiny room, a symphony of desire and desperation. Mia's cries drove me wild, her nails raking down my spine, sending shivers through my body. I was drowning in her depths, knowing that if she walked away, I'd be left with nothing but heartache.

At this moment, I knew my heart had claimed her and Michael. And even though the world outside was threatening to tear everything down, I wanted nothing more than to keep her forever.

"Antonio," she whispered, her voice breathy and filled with longing. Her whisper was my undoing. I pounded into her, driving my cock to places even she didn't know existed. Her body bucked against mine in a steady rhythm. Time seemed to stand still as her walls locked down and gripped my shaft.

My vision blurred, and my heart thudded with a fury of emotions as I lost control, tumbling into the abyss right alongside her. With every shudder of her body, my essence spilled into her, filling her to the brim. The warmth of my seed seeping out where our bodies joined brought me back to the reality of what we had just done.

"Mia, baby… I forgot to use a condom," I murmured, a hint of panic in my voice.

She cupped my cheek with such tenderness, her smile soothing my fears. "I'm on the pill and haven't been with anyone but the two of you. Plus, this isn't the first time we've forgotten about one. It's okay, Antonio. I enjoy feeling you and Michael inside me, skin on skin."

I searched her face for any sign of regret but found none. "I didn't realize…" I stammered, shocked this wasn't the first time I'd lost myself completely in the moment.

The pilot came over the intercom, announcing our descent into London, interrupting any more conversation about what we'd shared.

"We should get cleaned up." I pressed a kiss to Mia's head. "We need to get seated and buckle up for landing. Come on, let me help you."

I held out my hand and tugged her to her feet. Seeing the remnants of our lovemaking dripping down her leg made me feel possessive. It was evidence that Mia was really mine. After helping her get dressed and sharing a few more kisses, we found ourselves seated in the cabin.

She stared out the window, watching the skyline meet the ground as we landed. As I suspected, we didn't remain grounded for long. Mia leaned her head against me and closed her eyes. We should have crawled back to the bed, but exhaustion had plagued us, and my eyes drifted shut as well. I thought of Michael as the remaining tendrils of alertness faded into the dark.

When this was over... I would make them both mine *permanently.*

143

seventeen

ANTONIO

ONE WEEK. That's how long Mia and I had been in Italy. We spent our days exploring the countryside, trying to distract ourselves from the gnawing guilt over leaving Vegas —and more specifically, Michael.

Nothing had changed in Vincenzo's condition, and I was going stir-crazy with worry. The longer he remained unconscious, the lower his chances of recovery became. Dmitri's silence was worrisome, adding another layer to my anxiety. The media had classified Mia as a missing person, and the world believed her residence had been lost with her body unrecovered. Her boss, Mike Donovan, was still in hiding, stalling the case against Riley. The FBI had turned their attention to the Prizrak, temporarily forgetting about my family.

Mia pressed her lips to my neck and wrapped her arms around my waist, her touch a soothing balm to my frayed nerves. "What are you thinking?"

"I hate that my brother is still not awake. I hate that you have to stay missing. I hate that my sister-in-law might have those babies alone. But most of all… I hate not having Michael here.”

“I hate it, too,” she whispered. Her voice was trembling with shared anguish. “But this will be over soon. Maybe it's time we go back.”

“No.” I turned to face her, my heart aching at the thought. “It isn't safe yet. I can't stand that my brother is lying unconscious or that we're separated from Michael, but if something were to happen to you… I wouldn't come back from that.”

I held her against my chest, pressing my lips to her head. The past few days had been a whirlwind of emotions. I missed Michael more than I admitted, but she knew. Mia had learned to read my emotions better than my family, almost better than Michael himself.

“I miss Michael,” Mia murmured, startling me from my thoughts.

We FaceTimed with him every day, sometimes more than once, but it wasn't enough.

“When this is all over, we'll take a vacation.”

“I know.” Mia kicked at the sand as we walked along the shore, the waves gently lapping at our feet. Suddenly, she stopped and covered her mouth. “I'm going to be sick.” She dropped my hand and turned toward the water, her body shaking as she heaved the contents of her stomach into the sea.

I rubbed her back, trying to provide some comfort. “Are you okay?”

“I think I ate something bad. Can we go home?”

"Yeah." I took her hand and led her back to the car. After helping her into the passenger seat, I climbed in and started the engine. I couldn't help staring at her as I eased the car onto the road. Her face was pale, and a deep worry gnawed at my gut.

"Do you want me to call the family doctor? He can meet us at the house."

"No. I think I just need to lie down." She rested her head against the cool glass and closed her eyes.

"If you still feel bad after a nap, I'm calling him." I raised my brow, daring her to argue. She must have realized I wasn't playing around because she closed her eyes and kept quiet.

Once we got back to my parents' estate, I helped her to our room and tucked her into bed. She continued to insist she just needed rest. I closed the door and headed down to the study, unable to shake the feeling something was wrong with her—maybe some lingering effects of her ordeal earlier in the week, but I pushed the concern down.

The vibration in my pocket derailed the negative thoughts consuming me. Michael's face filled the screen. It was odd for him to be calling me at this hour. It was only eight in the morning back in Vegas.

"Michael?" I pressed the phone to my ear and held my breath, dreading the worst.

"He's awake."

My ears rang with his words as my vision swam in front of me. I stumbled forward, crashing my knee into the desk. "What did you say?"

"Vincenzo is awake."

I dropped into the chair, a sob escaping my lips. My brother was awake. Ivanov had failed to kill him. "How is he?"

"He's Vin. The doctors said if his tests come back okay this morning, he'll go home later today."

"I wish I was there." The guilt crept in, twisting my insides as I thought of my brother back home.

"I know. He keeps asking where you are. Massimo said once he gets settled at home, he'll bring them both up to speed. For now—"

"I know," I cut him off, the frustration evident in my voice. "I shouldn't call him. He'd get it out of me because I don't think I have it in me to lie to him anymore."

"How's Mia?" Michael asked, concern lacing his tone.

"She's sleeping. We were down at the beach, and she got sick."

"You seem… worried about something," Michael noted, his perceptive nature always a step ahead. "Did you have the doctor look at her?"

"She refused. You know she's as stubborn as a mule."

"Yeah, that's true. If she isn't better in a day or two, call him anyway."

"I will." I sighed, feeling the weight of the world on my shoulders. "I miss you, Michael. We miss you."

"Same here. I'm hoping with the news of Vincenzo's release, Ivanov will slip up and make a move."

"Is he safe?"

"That's a dumb question. You know your brother. Massimo has recruited some of Miguel's men to protect the entire family. They're also helping to locate the missing guns."

"Any luck on that front?" I squeezed the bridge of my nose, the tension building.

"Donny said they have some leads."

"Let me know what you find."

"And you let me know how Mia is. I'll call later this afternoon so I can talk to her. Maybe if I ask, she'll let the doctor check her out."

I laughed, knowing he was probably right. She missed him enough to do whatever he asked. "All right. I'll talk to you later. Please give everyone my love."

"I will. I love you and Mia. Tell her, will you?"

"Of course. I love you, too."

I leaned back in the desk chair, running my hands through my hair. Now that Vin was awake, things would move fast. Ivanov would likely lash out, knowing he hadn't killed my brother. And since Mia was tucked away with me here, I worried about who would be the one to feel his wrath.

"Antonio?" The shrill sound of my sisters echoed through the house.

"In here," I called out as I stood to greet them.

Carmela pulled me into a hug. "Have you heard?"

"Yes, Michael just called me."

"I'm relieved. Celestina and I were about to use the plane to go to the States. Now we can wait until the morning." Carmela smiled, but her eyes were still clouded with concern.

"No. You need to stay here. Your presence in Vegas would create a complication they don't need right now."

"What? Are you serious? I'm tired of being told no, Antonio. We weren't allowed to go when he got stabbed. And now he's awake, and we still can't go?" Celestina folded her arms across her chest, her frustration mirroring my own.

"Ivanov could use you against Vincenzo. You know that. I want to be there, too, but I know it's safer for me to be here."

"Right… because of Mia." Carmela rolled her eyes. "Where is the little woman?"

"Upstairs sleeping. She isn't feeling well."

"Is she pregnant?" Celestina laughed at her own joke, but her words hit me like a freight train.

I held my sister's gaze, her words rolling around in my head. Could she be pregnant? Lord knows we have had plenty of sex, even before we came to Italy.

"Holy shit. You're thinking about it, aren't you?"

"I mean—"I ran my palm down my face and sighed, "it's not impossible."

"Jesus Christ. What is it with the Anastasi men and accidental pregnancies?"

"It could be Michael's just as much as it could be mine."

That seemed to sober the twins up. They both stared at me wide-eyed as my words resonated with them.

"She needs to see a doctor." Carmela pointed at me. "You should make her."

"I can't make her do anything, Carm. She's a grown adult, not to mention wildly stubborn. But when she wakes up, I'll talk to her. In the meantime," I walked past them toward the kitchen. "You two hungry?"

He followed me, and we settled at the kitchen table. As I prepared some snacks, the gravity of everything weighed on me. My brother's awakening was a miracle, but the battle wasn't over. With Mia possibly pregnant and Ivanov still a looming threat, the storm was far from passing. The momentary relief gave way to the persistent dread of the unknown, but I knew one thing for sure—I would protect those I loved no matter the cost.

eighteen

MICHAEL

SOMETHING WAS WRONG. I tugged at my hands that were bound behind my back. My head felt like a weighted balloon as I tried to regain control of my faculties. Tiny dots swam through my vision as I blinked the fog from my eyes and forced them open. The inside of my mouth felt like it was stuffed full of cotton, even though it wasn't.

When the haze clouding my vision finally cleared, I realized I was tied to a chair in what appeared to be a basement. The walls were made of gray cinder blocks, and the floor was cold, unforgiving concrete. It had only one window near the ceiling of the room, and it could barely be classified as a window. It appeared to be a two-by-four rectangle with bars on the opening, offering no hope of escape or sunlight.

I wiggled, trying to loosen my hands, but the movement sent a lightning bolt of pain up my arm. When I glanced down, I could see the pool of blood gathering beneath the chair. What the hell was going on? Panic began to set in, my heart racing as I struggled to piece together my fractured memories. The last thing I recalled was walking out of the hospital after

Vincenzo was released. Massimo had put him in his car, and I told him I would be by later. Then I got in my car—at least, I think I did.

"Ah, I see you're awake." The thick Russian accent sent chills through my veins. "I bet you're wondering where you are and how you got here?"

The overhead light came on, bathing me in a harsh fluorescent glow. I squinted, trying to shield my eyes from the painful brightness.

"Ivanov?" I gritted my teeth, pulling against my restraints. "How?" My voice was a mix of anger and fear, the taste of bile rising in my throat. "How did you manage this?"

"One of my men was waiting in your car. You didn't even notice him lying in the backseat. Nor did you fight when he jabbed the needle in your neck." He stepped closer, his presence overwhelming. "I was surprised your bodyguard didn't put up more of a fight when his throat was slit."

I closed my eyes and hissed, the reality of his words sinking in. One of Miguel's men had been assigned to watch over me. And now… he was dead. My fault. All my fault.

"They'll come for me," I said, trying to inject confidence into my voice, though it wavered with doubt.

"You'll be dead. I'm not using you as bait, Mr. Brighton. I'm using you as a catalyst."

"A catalyst?" I furrowed my brow, confusion mixing with dread.

"When I dump your remains at the doorstep of the Anastasi family, your lover will be beside himself with rage. He'll slip up, giving me the opportunity to kill them all. Imagine —the entire line of Anastasi men gone. My life will be mine again, and I can continue doing what I do best—controlling others."

The weight of his words crashed down on me. I watched as the door opened, and several men stormed in. My breaths quickened with the knowledge these men were here to torture me. Somehow, I'd become a pawn in Ivanov's sick game. Ivanov was right… Antonio would be blinded by grief and do something stupid, putting everyone at risk, including Mia. My heart squeezed with the realization I would never see her again.

Ivanov set up a camera in the corner and motioned to a man standing off to the side. "Go ahead. Have your fun. When you're done, kill him. I want the Anastasi family to see I mean business."

Ivanov walked out, leaving me alone with the three men. I watched as one of them lifted a duffle bag and set it on a table against the wall. Nothing good was going to come from this. Even if I survived, which was unlikely, the undiluted rage Antonio would experience would be catastrophic.

"Drag him over here," one of the Russians ordered.

I was unceremoniously dragged across the concrete floor in the chair. The chair tipped forward, leaving me face down on the hard ground. My cheek felt as though it shattered into a million fragments, blinding me in pure agony. His helper launched his foot into my ribcage, adding to the blistering pain. His boot connected with my flesh, the steel tip tearing at the skin. The air in my lungs whooshed out, making me certain he had just cracked my ribs.

"Why are you doing this?" I hissed, knowing their response before the words spilled from their mouths.

"Shut up."

Another blow to my side had me seeing stars. As darkness threatened to consume me, I conjured up the images of Antonio and Mia. I prayed they knew how much I loved them. If I could come back to them, I would. We hadn't gotten enough time together, so this couldn't possibly be the end.

I was flipped over, my hands crushed beneath the back of the metal chair. My body shuddered as my shirt was ripped from my flesh and the tip of a knife pressed into my skin. Nothing could have prepared me for the pain. My scream echoed off the walls of the room as the blade carved into the meat covering my heart. As much as I wanted to live for Antonio, I wasn't sure I could. The last thing I felt was the weight of something heavy coming down on my knee. The blistering anguish it caused sent me into the darkness I had been teetering on.

But before the darkness could fully claim me, I felt a surge of determination. No, this couldn't be the end. I couldn't let it be. For Antonio, for Mia, for everyone who counted on me— I had to fight. I had to survive, if only to give them a chance.

The heavy boot came down on my knee again, the sickening crunch echoing in the room. My scream was raw, primal, tearing through my throat. But amid the pain, I found a spark of defiance. I focused on it, let it grow, let it fuel me.

"You think…this will break me?" I spat through gritted teeth, glaring up at my captors. "You're… dead wrong."

The man with the knife smirked, clearly amused by my defiance. He knelt beside me, the blade glinting in the harsh light. "You're tougher than you look, I'll give you that. But everyone breaks eventually."

His words were a taunt, a promise of more pain to come. But I latched onto the thought of Antonio, of Mia, of the life I still had to fight for. I couldn't let Ivanov win. I wouldn't let him destroy everything I loved.

The man brought the knife down again, this time carving a deep, deliberate line across my chest. I screamed again, the sound raw and jagged, but I refused to let go of that spark. I clung to it with everything I had, willing myself to stay conscious, to stay defiant.

"Ivanov…will never…win," I gasped, my voice barely more than a whisper. "Antonio… will come…and he'll…destroy you."

The man laughed, a cold, mirthless sound. "We'll see about that," he said, standing up and looking down at me with a mixture of contempt and curiosity. "But for now, let's see how much more you can take."

They continued their assault, each blow, each cut pushing me closer to the edge of consciousness. But I held on, driven by a fierce determination to survive. I wouldn't let them break me. I couldn't.

Hours seemed to pass, or maybe it was just minutes. Time lost all meaning in the haze of pain and darkness. But eventually, the men grew tired, their movements slowing. One of them grabbed a phone, taking pictures of my battered body, likely to send as proof to Ivanov.

"Enough for now," he said, his voice a dull roar in my ears. "He'll be back to finish you off later."

They left me there, alone in the cold, dark basement. The pain was overwhelming, my body a mass of bruises and cuts, but I was still alive. And as long as I was alive, there was hope.

I took a ragged breath, my vision swimming as I focused on the small window high up on the wall. The bars seemed impenetrable, but beyond them, I could see a sliver of the night sky. The stars twinkled faintly, a reminder that there was still a world out there, still a chance.

With every ounce of strength I had left, I vowed to survive. For Antonio, for Mia, for the fight that was yet to come. I would endure this. I would escape. And when I did, Ivanov would pay for every moment of pain, for every drop of blood spilled.

This wasn't the end. It was just the beginning. And I would make sure that when the final battle came, it would be Ivanov who lay broken and defeated.

I'm sorry.

The thought whispered through my mind as my body betrayed me and gave in to the darkness beckoning me. This was going to change everything.

This... was going to start a war unlike anything anyone had ever seen before.

nineteen

MIA

I STRETCHED my arms above my head and yawned. The sky had finally given way to the dark, confirming I had slept for a while. I slipped from the bed and padded my way downstairs in search of Antonio. His sisters' laughter made me smile. They'd welcomed me with open arms when we arrived. Carmela and Celestina were the youngest of the Anastasi siblings and had been home on break for the last couple of weeks. I was worried they would resent my presence, but we hit it off.

"I see you're awake." Antonio rose from the kitchen table and tugged me into his arms. "How are you feeling?"

"Better. I think the sun and something I ate got to me." I glanced at Carmela, who was refilling her wineglass. "Are we celebrating?" I cocked my head in confusion.

"Yes." Antonio led me to the table and sat down, pulling me into his lap. "Vincenzo woke up last night."

"What?" I searched his eyes, seeing the pure elation

reflecting in them. "That's wonderful. And everything's okay?"

"Yes. In fact—" Antonio handed me a full glass, "He got to go home today. Massimo called me and said his tests all came back normal. No brain damage or throat damage. He's resting comfortably in his own bed with his wife." He clinked his glass against mine.

"Is that a good idea?" Celestina pointed to the glass now pressed against my lips.

I paused, dropping the glass from my mouth. "Is there a problem with me having a glass in celebration?"

"If you're pregnant, there is." Carmela chuckled as she swallowed down the remnants of the liquid pooling in her own glass.

"Excuse me?" I glanced at the girls. "Pregnant? Where would you get such an idea?"

"You got sick."

"Lots of people get sick. That doesn't make them pregnant." I glared back at Antonio. "Did you tell them that?"

"No." He set his glass down and raised his palms in defense. "It was all them. I just told them you were sick today. They jumped to that conclusion on their own. But Mia—" he tugged my hand in his, "could you be?"

"No." I pushed up from his lap and walked to the sink. Bracing my palms against the edge of the counter, I blew out a breath. "I couldn't be." Even as I said the words, a trickle of doubt hummed in the back of my mind.

"Maybe—" Antonio paused mid-sentence as the phone vibrating across the table caught his attention. "Hey, Big Brother." Antonio reached out, holding his hand out for me to take. As I went to grab it, his arm dropped, and he stood abruptly. "What?" The sharp tone in his voice made my hair stand on end.

I stepped forward, placing my hand on his arm. "What is it, Antonio?" I could tell by his rigid stance something was wrong.

"I don't understand what you're telling me." He fisted his hair with his free hand. "I thought you had guards on everyone."

Celestina and Carmela stood, crowding closer to listen. We needed to know what was happening, but Antonio only paced the floor.

"No, I don't give a fuck, Massimo. We're coming home tonight. Fuck that, Brother. I won't wait in Italy while he's missing."

My breath caught in my chest at his admission. Someone was missing, and I prayed it wasn't Vincenzo. Not this soon after being released from the hospital. I listened as Antonio discussed our departure plans with Massimo, knowing we would go back regardless of the dangers. He shoved the phone into his pocket and covered his face with his hands.

"Antonio?" I stepped closer and wrapped my arm around his body. "Who is it? Is it Vincenzo?" I was completely caught off guard by the look of torment when he finally turned toward me.

"No." His eyes cut to his sisters before coming back to meet mine. "It's Michael." His voice cracked. "Ivanov has him."

My ears seemed to go deaf as my body collapsed to the ground. Antonio was there, pulling me into his arms as the sob ripped from my lips.

"No!" I cried out. "You're wrong. He can't have him. He can't." My body shuddered from the emotion pouring out of me.

Antonio carried me through the kitchen and perched us both on the couch.

"Mia… look at me." His fingers pressed beneath my chin. I was being selfish. When I glanced into his eyes, his pain mirrored mine. The whites of his eyes were red and filled with unspent tears. "We're going home, and we're going to bring him back."

"How do you know? How…" I gasped, searching for the words.

"How do they know?" I nodded, unable to speak.

"Massimo won't tell me what he has, but something was sent to him, confirming Ivanov took Michael."

"He's going to kill him."

"Shhh." Antonio pulled me against his body. "We can't think like that."

But I could hear it in his voice. He didn't believe the words either. He knew the ruthless nature of Dmitri Ivanov first-hand. Had it not been for their friends in Chile, Antonio would be dead, and we wouldn't be sitting here.

"Antonio." Carmela stood before us. "I called the pilot. He's fueling the plane now. Come on, get up. Celestina and I will take you to the hangar."

Antonio nodded and stood, lifting me into his arms.

"I can walk."

"No, I need you close to me right now. Let me do this."

I nodded, snuggling into his arms. I needed him too. I was barely hanging on by a thread, and I knew at any moment, I'd shatter into a thousand pieces. Looking into his eyes, I knew he wasn't too far behind me from falling apart as well.

We boarded the plane forty minutes after getting the call. Eleven hours in the sky would feel like torture, making my stomach roll with unease. Sensing my discomfort, Antonio eased me into a seat.

"Sit down, Rach." We'd been in the air for a little over five hours, which meant six more to go. I hated this—hated every part of not already being home to wait for news.

"Massimo told me Michael's guard was found dead near his car." He plopped down across from me and fastened his belt. "Apparently, they nabbed him right there in the fucking parking lot." I hiccupped a sob, trying to hold it in for Antonio's sake. "I don't know if I can survive this, Mia. Michael is my world, and without him, I'll be half a man."

"You still have me." I blinked the tears from my eyes. "I love you, Antonio. That won't change if…" I couldn't bring myself to say it.

"If he's dead?" Antonio narrowed his eyes at me. "Don't think it. You hear me, Mia. Don't you ever say it again."

Antonio undid his seatbelt and stormed toward the tiny bedroom in the back.

I knew he was running high on emotions, but his callous response hurt me deeply. I curled in on myself and let the emotions run rampant. All I could think was that this was going to be the thing that ruined what Antonio and I had together. That thought made me feel so guilty—how selfish it was to be thinking of my own heart when Michael was out there being tortured or, worse, dead.

"Mia?" Antonio squatted down beside me. "I'm so fucking sorry." He broke, his eyes red with emotion as he cried. "I love you, and how I just acted, I…"

"I don't want to lose you too, Antonio." I slid from my perch and wrapped my arms around him. "I couldn't survive it if I lost both of you."

"I just need to hold you." He wrapped his arms around me and lifted us from the ground.

He carried me to the rear of the plane and laid us down on the bed. His arms wrapped around me, holding so tight against him, I felt his heart beating against my back. The silence and sound of our ragged breathing lulled us to sleep. This was going to test everything about our new relationship.

I just hoped it survived the carnage we'd be facing.

ANTONIO

MIA and I managed to rest for an hour but eventually emerged from the private bedroom and sat wordlessly until we landed. What could we say to each other? We both loved Michael and knew the outcome was likely going to leave us equally devastated. Ivanov was not the type of man to negotiate. He'd taken Michael to prove a point. Massimo suspected he was trying to bait me into losing my shit, and truth be told, I was close.

"Mia." I brushed my hand down her hair. Even in the early morning light, her golden strands glimmered under my touch. "We're here, baby."

She opened her eyes and fumbled with her seatbelt. When she couldn't get it to unlatch, she screamed. I reached down and pressed the button, releasing its hold on her.

"Take a breath. I got you." I pulled her to her feet and wrapped her in my arms.

After coming unglued on her, I decided I needed to be more like Michael and be her rock. We were both hurting, but she needed me to be strong, and that was the only thing keeping me grounded. Otherwise, I was ready to go off half-cocked and likely get myself killed. That would leave her here alone —mourning both Michael and me.

Mourning.

My mind was already convinced he wasn't coming back because he was probably dead, and that thought gutted me. Massimo and Madison waited at the bottom of the steps. Massimo pulled me into a hug while Madison comforted Mia. Her sobs tore at my soul, fracturing what little of my heart remained. I didn't know how much I had left in me.

Once we were all seated in the SUV, Massimo turned toward me.

"We found where they were holding him, but the building was empty."

"How do you know it was the right place?"

"We just know." Massimo glanced over at Mia, who was pressed against my side. Madison held his hand, watching our every move. "They've either moved him or already dumped his body."

Mia let out a whimper, her body shaking with the pain I was trying to hide. I squeezed her hand in mine as I spoke.

"Has Ivanov made any demands?"

"No. Which is why I think this was an attempt to lure one of us out. Some of our contacts have heard murmurings on the streets that he wants to enrage you and start a war."

"Isn't there already a war happening?" I grunted, glancing out the window as I responded.

"To some extent, yes, but he wants to eradicate our family from Vegas, and likely Italy, too. The only way to do that is to kill us all."

"Fuck."

"Exactly. Which is why I need you to keep a level head as much as you can. Can you do that for me, *fratello*?"

I glanced over at Mia and pressed my lips to her head.

"For her, yes. I can't risk leaving her or losing her. So, his plan backfired."

Massimo nodded his head in understanding.

"The good news is we're all going to Vincenzo's place. Madison and I have been staying there with him and Riley. It makes protecting everyone easier."

"How is he handling everything?"

"As you would expect. He wants Ivanov's head on a platter." Massimo smirked. "But Riley refuses to let him get out of bed. She told him he was going to be on bed rest with her until the doctor gave him the all-clear. Which won't happen for a few more weeks."

"That's probably good for Ivanov. Having an Anastasi pissed off is never a good thing. Having La Lama enraged is far worse. Vin, being laid up, will buy him some time."

"True." Massimo turned his eyes back on the road. "But he doesn't just have us to deal with. He has pissed off the Sureños and the Silvas. Matias offered to send some men here to help if necessary. He wants Ivanov dead just as much as us… if not more."

"That's good." I gripped Mia against my side as we drove toward Vincenzo's.

I wanted to burn down the world to save Michael, but for now, Mia needed me. For her sake—and mine—I hoped we would find him.

"We're here." I glanced up to find us parking in front of Vincenzo's house. There were armed guards everywhere, making me shudder with rage. This was Ivanov's doing. Our lives had been turned upside down because of one man.

"Come on, baby." I helped Mia from the car and guided her through the door. "Let's get you inside." Vincenzo was standing at the foot of the stairs, his expression matching my own.

"Antonio." He wrapped his body around mine and hugged me tight. I lost the control I had and let the tears fall. "I got you, brother. I got you."

My body shook with the emotions pouring out of me. Vin just held me, his hand patting my back. Mia gripped my hand in hers, her own tears falling. I hated to be so weak in front of her, but the truth was, my heart was missing right along with hers.

"We're going to find him, *fratello*. I promise you. Ivanov is going to pay for this."

I pulled back and wiped my face off. Mia pressed against me, her arms wrapping around my waist.

"Vin, this is Mia."

He cocked an eyebrow in question. "The woman who was trying to put my wife in prison?"

"Vin." Riley's voice seemed to relax his rigid stance. "She's not the enemy anymore. Mia—" she leaned into Vin's arms and smiled, "It's nice to finally meet you."

"Riley. I'm so sorry this is happening."

"Pfft." Riley blew out a breath. "It's not your fault. Dmitri Ivanov has been fucking with this family for a long time now. I'm sad it wasn't him I killed."

I watched Mia's expression as she processed Riley's words. She seemed to find a measure of comfort in Riley's straight-forwardness, the way she faced the brutal reality without flinching. It was a strength Mia needed to see right now, and I was grateful for Riley's presence.

"Riley, let's get something straight. You didn't kill Dmitri's brother. He did." She pointed at Vincenzo. "Frankly, I don't care. Both men deserve death. And I no longer work for the D.A.'s office—at least I won't soon enough. I plan to resign now that I'm back home. My choice was made the moment I gave my heart to your brother and Michael." Her voice cracked with emotion when she spoke his name. She cleared her voice and continued. "Let's not pretend anymore. Your family has my unwavering support."

Riley glanced at Vincenzo, who was standing there with an unreadable expression. She smiled and blew out a breath.

"All right then. No secrets. Let's get you two situated. It's going to be a long couple of days."

We followed her up the steps and into the spare room. I couldn't help but smile at her rounded belly as she left us alone and headed back to her room.

Mia removed her clothes and crawled onto the bed. She drew her knees to her chest and stifled a sob. I kicked my shoes off and stripped down to my boxers before crawling in beside her. I wanted to take her pain away, but I didn't even know what to do with my own.

I listened to her cry herself to sleep, each sob and shudder of her body another reminder of the gravity of our situation. Sleep was impossible, even with her snuggled against my back. My head was all over the place. With as little movement as I could muster, I slid from the bed and pulled on some sweatpants. I needed to clear my head. Kissing Mia on the head, careful not to wake her, I slipped out of the room. I found myself in the kitchen, staring blankly out the back window. Michael was somewhere out there, and it was killing me not to be out looking for him.

"Can't sleep?" Vincenzo's voice interrupted my thoughts.

"No. What about you? Shouldn't you be in bed resting?"

"Probably, but like you, I couldn't sleep." Vincenzo pulled a bottle of whiskey from the cabinet and filled two glasses. "Here." He slid the amber liquid across the table and sat down. Setting the whiskey bottle on the table in front of himself, he smiled. "Have a drink. It'll help."

I slid into the chair opposite him. The burn from the alcohol felt good going down. "That was good. Thanks."

"So… you and the prosecutor?" Vincenzo swirled his glass and stared at me.

I held his gaze. "Yeah." I knew he suspected more, but telling Vin I was bisexual scared the shit out of me. "Is that going to be a problem?"

"Not anymore. Riley tells me she is trying to help end this circus of a trial. And hearing it out of her mouth tonight made me see her differently." Vin grabbed the whiskey, refilled his glass, and slid the bottle to me. "But why do I feel like there is more you're afraid to say?"

"Because there is." I filled my glass and downed the liquor.

"So, spit it out, Antonio. I've known for a while you've been keeping something from us. I've bitten my tongue, knowing you would tell me in your own time, but time's up. Does this have to do with the missing attorney?"

I took a deep breath and closed my eyes for a moment. I shouldn't have been so scared to tell him who I was—but his opinion mattered more to me than anyone else in the family.

"I am in love with Mia." He eyed me quizzically, waiting for the words I held back. "But I'm also in love with Michael."

Vincenzo's eyebrows pinched in thought. He shook his head, and I assumed he was trying to make sense of what I had said. When his gaze finally met mine, I was stunned because all I saw was love.

"I figured as much. Why are you just now telling me? Why hide it?"

I blew out my breath. "I've been in love with him for a while but fought my feelings… out of fear."

"Fear of what we would think?" He asked matter-of-factly. "You know that's stupid, right? That we would turn our backs on you because of your sexual preferences. Wait…" Vincenzo smiled. "Grandfather knew, didn't he?"

"He did. Somehow, he figured it out. Grandfather thought I was being irrational about coming out… turns out he was right. All this time, I hid who I was because I didn't want to disappoint the family when the only person I was disappointing was me."

"Explain to me how this works. You love Michael and Mia, and they're okay with the arrangement?"

"As unconventional as it is, yes. Mia loves him as much as she loves me. She's fucked up over Michael's disappearance. I'm trying to be strong for her, but my heart is breaking, too. Why did this happen when I finally found the courage to tell everyone how I feel—only to have lost him for good?"

Vincenzo stood and moved around the table. He squatted beside my chair and pulled me into a hug.

"As long as I have a breath in my body, I will find him, *fratello*. Nothing about you would ever change how important you are to me. And if you love a man and a woman, then we'll love them, too. That's what family does—we lift each other up in difficult times, not just the good ones."

For the first time since being a grown adult, I cried in my brother's arms. His acceptance was something I didn't know I needed. Hearing him say the words and promise to bring Michael home were the final fractures in my resolve. I was lost, knowing Michael was missing, but with the support of my brothers and the love of Mia, maybe there was hope.

Hope I could *survive* the pain.

Hope I could *have* a future.

But most of all… Hope that there would be an ending that wouldn't *crush* me.

twenty-one

MIA

TIME SEEMED to stand still for what felt like an eternity. It had been two weeks since we had returned to Vegas. Vincenzo and Riley had welcomed us into their home, along with Massimo and Madison. I was grateful for them because they tried to keep Antonio and me from falling apart. The only positive thing to come out of Michael's kidnapping was that the FBI had stopped pursuing a case against Riley. My former boss was still in protective custody and was also considering leaving the job. Agent Jackson was sitting around Massimo's desk, talking to him and Vincenzo. Their voices were low, making it difficult to hear from where I was standing. Whatever evidence they had that proved Ivanov had taken Michael had been kept away from Antonio and me. That thought pissed me off and had me stepping into their office to demand answers.

The three men stopped speaking and turned to look at me. "Mia, is Antonio okay?" Vincenzo leaned forward in his chair, looking for his brother behind me.

"He's fine. Riley's doctor gave him a sleeping pill because he hasn't been sleeping." I ran my fingers through my hair and sighed. "I want to see the proof."

Massimo tilted his head. "Proof?"

Agent Jackson visibly paled and stiffened in his seat. He knew me almost as well as Antonio did, seeing as we'd been close partners for nearly a decade. I was certain he understood what I was asking for, even if the other two wanted to pretend they didn't.

"Yes, the proof." I held Massimo's gaze and lifted my chin. "I know you received something that alerted you Ivanov had Michael. I want to see it."

"Mia." The sound of Vincenzo's chair scraping the wooden floor echoed off the walls. "You're going to have to trust us."

"I do, but I need to see it for myself. Nothing has happened in weeks. If Ivanov has him, why isn't he making threats or demands?"

"Come." Vincenzo pressed his hand to my shoulder. "Sit." He guided me to the chair he had been sitting in. He slowly kneeled in front of me and pulled my hands into his. "I know this is awful. I would be crazy if it was Riley or anyone I loved. But you have to understand, we aren't sharing that detail with you. You have to trust that it's to protect you and Antonio."

"Antonio what?" My eyes found Antonio in the doorway, looking just as disheveled as he was earlier. "What's going on here?"

"Mia wants to see the evidence we have proving Ivanov has Michael."

Antonio froze, the realization he'd not seen it yet himself clear on his face.

"I want to see it, too."

"*Fratello.*" Massimo stood and stepped toward Antonio—who moved away from his reach.

"No, Mia's right. We deserve to see whatever it is Ivanov sent to you. Please."

Letting go of Vincenzo's hand and pushing to my feet, I went to Antonio and wrapped my arms around his waist.

The men shared an expression of terror before Agent Jackson spoke.

"I understand why you need to see it, Antonio." He sighed, giving me a sympathetic look. "Mia, however, shouldn't."

Antonio glanced down at me and furrowed his brow. "No, she deserves the truth as much as I do. We both love him."

"I don't like this," Vincenzo said as he stood. "It isn't something either of you should see, *fratello*. Are you sure this is wise?" He glanced back at Massimo, who was shaking his head.

"Yes. I appreciate you trying to protect us, but if I… no, we are going to accept he probably isn't coming home, we need to know everything."

"Fine." Massimo ran his hand down his face. "Antonio, promise me you won't lose it and go off on your own and do something stupid."

"He won't." I tightened my hand on Antonio's. "I won't let him."

"Follow me." Massimo headed toward the security room in Vincenzo's house, Vincenzo and Agent Jackson following close behind. "I think Antonio needs to see it first." He gave his brother a knowing look.

"Okay." Antonio stepped forward, letting go of my hand. "Wait here, Mia."

"What? No. We're going to look together."

"Please. If it's as bad as they are making me feel it is, I don't want you to look."

I watched Vincenzo and Jackson as they stepped in behind Antonio, taking a protective stance at his backside. Massimo pulled out an iPad and pressed a few buttons.

"This was sent to us through an encrypted email. Alec has been trying to locate its origin but has had no luck. Antonio." Massimo held the tablet against his chest. "You need to prepare yourself."

ANTONIO NODDED, HIS FACE A MASK OF STOIC determination, but I could see the fear in his eyes. Massimo handed him the iPad, and Antonio's hands trembled slightly as he took it. The room was silent except for the faint hum of the air conditioning. I watched as the man I loved crumpled before my eyes. Massimo set the tablet down and dropped to the floor, grasping his brother. Vincenzo was beside them, his arms wrapped around Antonio as he shattered into a million pieces.

"No… No…" His voice broke, and he dropped the tablet onto the table, covering his face with his hands. "He's torturing him. That bastard is torturing Michael."

I rushed forward. Agent Jackson turned back to me. His eyes widened with shock when he realized what I was doing. I needed to see for myself. I needed to know what put Antonio on the ground. We moved at the same time, but my fingers wrapped around the device and snatched it off the table.

"Mia," Jackson hollered, but my body was on autopilot.

Nothing in my life prepared me for what was on the screen. Michael was lying sideways on what appeared to be a concrete floor. He was strapped to a chair, his hands bloody and twisted at an odd angle. Although his face was a bloody mess and hardly human anymore, I knew. My heart was lying helplessly on the floor.

A silent scream tore from my lips as the tablet slipped from my grasp and clattered to the floor. The sound seemed to echo in the room, but it was distant, like it was happening in another world. My world was collapsing, a rushing sound filling my ears, drowning out everything else. I could vaguely hear someone shouting my name, but it was as if they were miles away. Tiny pinpricks of black began to dot my vision, spreading like ink in water, as the world around me started to close in.

I couldn't breathe. My chest felt as though it was being crushed by an invisible force, a pain so intense and foreign that I was convinced I was having a heart attack. The ache radiated through my body, every beat of my heart sending a wave of agony through my veins. My lungs refused to draw in air, each attempt feeling like I was inhaling shards of glass.

Nothing was in focus. Faces, walls, furniture—all blurred together in a smudge of colors and shapes. The room tilted, my balance slipping away from me as if I was standing on the edge of a cliff, teetering. My legs gave out, and I tumbled forward, my body colliding with the edge of the desk. The sharp pain that echoed through my hip was almost a relief, a momentary distraction from the crushing torment in my chest.

I fell to the floor in a heap, my body a tangled mess of limbs and despair. The cold surface against my cheek was the only anchor to reality, but even that was slipping away. Darkness crept in at the edges of my vision, the black pinpricks merging into a suffocating void. The pain, both physical and emotional, was overwhelming, swallowing me whole. The last thing I was aware of was the feeling of someone's arms around me, their voice a distant murmur, before the darkness took over completely.

"I have you, Mia."

twenty-two

ANTONIO

I WATCHED AS MIA SLEPT. To anyone else, she looked like she was sleeping peacefully, but I knew otherwise. Her soft whimpers and the twitching of her body told me she was fighting the demons, even in her sleep. Had I listened to Massimo, she wouldn't be having nightmares. Hell, we wouldn't be having nightmares.

Every time I closed my eyes, I saw him lying there, broken, and battered, on that concrete floor. It's why I fought to sleep and refused sleeping pills, although I was thankful Mia had agreed to take them. Now, here I sat, watching her fight the monsters in her head.

"We found the guns," Massimo whispered as he stepped into the room. "Miguel's men intercepted a transport and kept the driver alive. I'm headed to the club now. He has him there, waiting for Vincenzo and me to arrive."

"I'm coming with you." I pushed to my feet and pressed a kiss to Mia's temple, my lips lingering, hoping she felt my presence even in her tormented dreams.

Massimo pressed his palm to my shoulder. "You don't have to."

"I know, but I need to do this for her."

Massimo tipped his chin in understanding and cupped my shoulder. "I'll call Catarina over to check on her."

"Thank you."

I walked through the house like a zombie, forcing a smile at Riley, who sat next to Vincenzo with her feet propped up on the table. She was due any day now, reminding me how long Michael had been gone.

"I'm going to go sit with her." Riley stood and pressed her hand to her back. "Lord knows I can't do anything else. Go." She sighed, waving her hand at the three of us. "See if you can get info about Michael."

"I'll be back." Vincenzo pressed a kiss to her cheek and patted her round belly. "Drew is right outside if you need something."

Riley ambled up the steps as we headed out the door and climbed into the awaiting SUV. Freddy, Massimo's driver, cranked the engine and headed toward the Velvet Ace Lounge and Casino. The silence in the car was thick. I knew there was a slim chance the man knew where Michael was or if he was even alive. And if he did, getting the information was going to be a challenge. Good thing I was ready to live up to the Anastasi name in a way I'd never done before.

We arrived at the club, thankful it was still early in the after-noon, leaving fewer patrons inside. Massimo keyed the code next to the basement door and waved us through. The room was filled with Miguel and several of his men when we stepped inside. In the center of the room, a man was tied to a metal chair. It was obvious Miguel and his guys had been less than kind to him, and for that, I was grateful.

Vincenzo moved in front of the man and grabbed his shirt. "Do you know who I am?"

The man's eyes widened in terror, his body trembling. "Y-yes," he stammered. "I know who you are—La Lama." He gasped, his eyes trying to focus on my brother. "I thought you were dead." His voice was raspy as he tried to breathe through what I assumed were broken ribs.

"I'm far from dead… but you—" Vin pulled his hair, tilting his head backward, "Are not. Tell me, where is the man you took from my family?"

"I-I don't know!" the man cried. his voice was high-pitched with fear. "Please, I don't know where he is!"

"Wrong answer," Vincenzo brought his elbow down, connecting the hard bone with the man's groin. He cried out, bucking against Vin's hold. "Try again. Where is Michael?"

"Gone."

I stumbled, my hand pressing into the table in the room. The pressure of Massimo's hand on my shoulder was the only thing reminding me to take deep breaths.

"Gone where?" Vincenzo slipped out the blade he had strapped to his belt and held it in front of the man's eyes. "This has been itching to carve up Ivanov. But he's not here. You are. He tried to take everything from my family, and you'll be the one to pay for his sins… for now." Vincenzo ran the steel down his shirt, causing the man to whimper. "Now, I can make this quick, or I can drag it out. It's up to you. Where is Michael Brighton?"

"They were going to take him and dump his body. That's all I know."

"He's dead?" I heard the words slip past my lips. The sound was bitter on my tongue as I tried to swallow the bile.

"I don't know. If he survived what Ivanov's henchmen did to him, I'd be surprised. I didn't have any part of that. I was only the mule for your weapons. Please… I have a family."

"Michael had a family," I growled as my feet moved of their own free will. My hands pulled the blade from Vincenzo's hands and drove it into the portly man's gut. My brother's eyes widened with surprise as he fought the knife from my palm.

The man's scream was guttural, his eyes bulging as he looked down at the knife protruding from his stomach. Blood seeped out, staining his shirt a deep crimson. His body convulsed, and he coughed, a splatter of blood landing on my face.

"Antonio!" Massimo's voice was sharp, but it barely registered. The only thing I could see was the image of Michael, battered and broken, lying helpless on that cold floor.

"Michael had a family," I repeated, my voice shaking with rage and sorrow. "And you took him from us. You don't get to plead for mercy. You don't get to cry for your family."

Vincenzo pulled me back, his grip firm but not harsh. "Antonio, we need him to talk. This isn't helping."

I stared at the man, watching as the life drained from his eyes. The rage that had fueled me moments ago now left me feeling hollow. My body trembled as I stepped back, the realization of what I had done washing over me.

"Antonio, look at me," Vincenzo said, his voice steady. "We'll find Michael. We'll get him back. But you need to stay in control. We can't lose you too."

He didn't have to say it. I knew what he meant. We would find Michael, dead or alive, and bring him home to us. I watched as Miguel's men wrapped Ivanov's man in a tarp and carried him from the room. Massimo whispered something to Miguel and nodded when he followed the guys out.

Vincenzo grabbed some towels and guided me to the small office attached to the massive room. He led me into the tiny shower my brother had installed specifically for cleanup purposes and turned on the water. The droplets washed over me, soaking my clothes to the bone. I watched in fascination as the water turned crimson and swirled around the drain, disappearing into the darkness below.

"Raise your arms." Vincenzo's voice drew me from the trance I had been in.

"What?" I blinked.

"Your shirt. Take it off. Massimo has some sweats for you to change into."

I glanced at the blood-splattered shirt, realizing for the first time what I had done. I wasn't the brother who inflicted violence, not like this. Sure, I had been in plenty of fights and had shot a few people, but something as personal as driving a knife into someone's gut—no. That was Vincenzo. Not me.

"What did I do?" My voice carried through the tiny shower as the steam filled the space.

"What you needed to do," Vincenzo said, reaching in and cutting off the water. "Take off your pants. They're soaked."

The denim made a sloshing sound as I pushed them down and let them pool at my feet. Most would find it weird that my brother was helping me undress, but we were family, and right now, I needed him. Deep down, I think he needed to be the one standing beside me. He wrapped a towel around me and helped me step out.

"Dry off. I'll grab the dry clothes."

It was as if I was caught in an alternate reality, unable to function independently. Vincenzo came back and handed me the sweatpants and shirt. Massimo leaned against the wall and watched as I pulled on the fresh clothes. He set a pair of shoes on the table and gave me a weak smile.

"These should fit you."

Nodding, I pulled them on. I closed my eyes and thought of Michael. Mia missed him fiercely, and so did I. We had only just begun to explore the love we had confessed to having—only to have it ripped away from us too soon.

"Hello?" Vincenzo's deep voice interrupted my thoughts. I watched as a myriad of emotions crossed his face. "We'll meet you there. Tell her I love her."

"What is it?" I glanced at him, worried something was wrong.

"Riley's water broke. Drew is driving them to the hospital."

"Them?"

"Mia is awake and with her. Let's go meet my babies."

If something good could come from this nightmare, it was my niece and nephew. I pushed down the disgust I felt burning at my core and followed my brothers out. For now, I needed to bury the fury coursing through my veins and focus on this one good thing.

After grabbing Madison from the office, we piled into the SUV. The drive to the hospital was a blur. My thoughts were a chaotic mix of worry for Michael and anticipation for the new lives about to enter our world. I tried to steady my breathing, to calm the storm inside me.

twenty-three

MIA

CAUGHT BETWEEN HEAVEN AND HELL, my dreams were filled with Michael. Some were blissful moments of happiness, while others were almost too torturous to bear. After nearly two months of no news and fighting the sleep, I knew I desperately needed help. Antonio had convinced me to take sleeping pills, and though I slept, it was not a restful slumber.

"Hey… there you are," Riley's soft voice said, lulling me from another nightmare. "You looked like you were having a bad dream. You all right?"

I pushed myself to a sitting position and glanced around the room, disoriented. "What time is it?"

"Around four. The guys had to go handle something at the club, so I promised to sit with you. Catarina was supposed to be here by now, but she's not answering her phone."

"Maybe she's working? Being an ER nurse can get hectic, and I'm sure she's tired of babysitting the likes of us."

"Yeah… if she was working, but she's off today. I was about to call Donny when you started crying in your sleep. Another nightmare?" She cocked her head, her expression filled with concern.

"Yeah. I have them a lot."

"I bet. I hate that you saw that video, Mia. No one should see their loved one like that."

My feet shifted off the edge of the bed and pressed into the wooden floor. For a moment, the room spun, and my stomach churned.

"Shit." I bolted toward the attached bathroom and heaved into the toilet.

"Mia?" Riley's voice whispered as she ran her hand down the back of my head. "Honey, could you be pregnant?"

I rested my head against the cool porcelain and drew in a breath.

"I don't know." It was the truth. "With everything going on, I lost track of my cycle. This isn't the first time I've been sick like this. When we were in Italy, I had a bout of sickness, and Antonio's sisters said the same thing. But then this…" My voice trailed off, unable to speak the words.

"When was your last period?"

My mind tried calculating when my last period was, the realization made me suck in a breath. "Before my house was blown up."

"That was almost four months ago." Riley patted my shoulder. "Come on, we need to have Drew take us to the store."

"Oh my God, Riley. I can't be pregnant right now."

"Why not?" She quirked a brow at me in question. "I know you're scared. Hell, I was too. But the truth is… this family is loyal and will love you no matter what. What has you so freaked out?"

"It could be either of theirs, Riley."

"And?" She followed me into the bedroom and huffed. "You love them both, right?"

"Yes." I answered without hesitation. I loved Antonio and Michael equally, each of them owning one half of my heart.

Riley smiled, her head tilting in question. "And they love each other and you, right?"

"Again… yes."

"Then there isn't a problem as far as I can tell." She shrugged her shoulders, "Antonio and Michael knew what they were signing up for when they decided you were part of the love they shared. This doesn't change a thing."

"But Michael's gone, and if it's his, he'll never know." A sob worked its way up my throat.

Riley pressed her hand against my shoulder. "Stop it, Mia. You may or may not have a part of a man you love inside you. Does it really matter who the father is? Would it change your love for either man?"

"No." I blew out a big breath and shook my head. "I'm just overwhelmed. This is not the best timing."

"Maybe it is." Riley patted my shoulder and started toward

the door. "Fuck." She grunted, causing me to tilt my head in alarm.

"Riley?" I glanced beneath her legs and realized there was a massive puddle of water forming between her legs. "Did your water just break?"

"Oh my God." Riley turned to look at me over her shoulder, her eyes wide with fear.

"Hey, it's all right. This is good, right? Let me get Drew. Seems like my problem can wait. We need to get you to the hospital."

Holding Riley's hand in mine, I helped her downstairs. Drew was standing near the door, looking at his cell phone. When he heard our approach, he looked up and paled.

"Holy shit, Riley. Mia, what's wrong?"

"Her water broke. Get the car and call the boys. They need to get Vincenzo to the hospital."

Drew sprang into action, his phone already at his ear as he rushed to get the car. Riley's grip on my hand tightened, and I could feel her anxiety mixing with my own. "Breathe, Riley," I murmured, trying to stay calm for both our sakes. "We'll get you there, and everything will be fine."

Riley winced as the first real contraction struck, forcing her to double over in pain. "Holy fuck," she whined, her breath whooshing out in response.

"It's okay. This is normal, and you're going to get to hold your beautiful babies in your arms today."

She pressed her hand to her back and held on to me as we

eased our way down the front steps to the waiting car. Drew ran around the back and pulled open the door.

"Vin's meeting us there."

We made our way outside, the cool night air hitting us like a wave. Drew pulled the car up to the curb, and I helped Riley into the backseat, her breathing becoming more labored with each contraction.

"Is this the first contraction you've felt?" Riley cut her eyes over to me, panic evident. "Riley, have you been having contractions all day?"

"I thought they were Braxton Hicks. Oh God." She closed her eyes and moaned, her grip on my fingers becoming painfully tight, confirming my worst fear. She was having contractions every few minutes.

"Drew, step on it! Or we're going to have the babies in this fucking car," I shouted, my own anxiety rising with each passing second.

"Don't think this is going to make me forget your minor issue. Madison was there for me when I found out, and now, it's my turn to be there for you. Holy cock balls!" Riley groaned with a strained voice.

Drew's expression was comical as he glanced in the rearview mirror, clearly freaked out at the possibility of delivering the babies himself. He didn't enjoy seeing Riley in pain and certainly didn't want to risk Vincenzo killing him if he had to look at her lady parts. Riley had been through enough over the last few months, and the last thing either of us wanted was for her to have these kids without her husband.

Somehow, miraculously, Drew had us at the hospital entrance in record time. Vincenzo and his brother were waiting when the car came to a stop. Vincenzo snatched the door open and scooped Riley out, his face a mask of determination and fear.

I slid from the car and walked straight into Antonio's arms. It didn't go unnoticed by me that his hair was damp, and he was dressed in sweats and a T-shirt.

"Everything okay?" I murmured against his chest, trying to draw strength from his presence.

"No, but it will be now that you're here," he replied, his voice trembling slightly. Realizing this man was holding on by a thread, just as I was, I decided I couldn't keep secrets from him.

"There's something we need to talk about, but it can wait until after the babies are born, okay?"

"What is it?" I could feel his heart speed up beneath my hand pressed against his chest.

"Nothing bad. Just surprising if I'm right, but it can wait. Right now, your brother needs us. Let's go and welcome your niece and nephew into the world. Then you can tell me why your hair is wet while we wait for them to be born."

I held his hand as we walked into the hospital. Madison had arrived and was sitting beside Massimo in the waiting room. Drew and Freddy were also propped against the wall, their faces etched with concern.

"Where's Catarina? Has anyone called her?" I glanced at the anxious faces. "Or your parents?"

"I called Gia and Gio," Madison smiled weakly. "They'll be here soon. But I couldn't get Catarina on the phone. I left a message."

"Let me call Donny." Massimo stood and pulled his phone out. We watched as he walked to the window looking out on the parking lot. His body tensed, and he ran his hand through his hair. Whatever Donny had told him, he wasn't happy about it.

"Massimo?" Madison sat up in the chair and reached out to him. "What is it?"

"It's Catarina. She's gone." Massimo turned, his face pale and grim. "Donny said she didn't show up for her shift today. They went to her apartment, and it's empty."

The weight of his words sank in, and I felt a fresh wave of panic. Catarina had been struggling with the family dynamics recently and I knew she was pissed about having Donny as her keeper... But missing—I couldn't wrap my head around it.

twenty-four

ANTONIO

"WHAT?" I jumped to my feet as my voice bellowed through the waiting room. "What do you mean, gone?"

Massimo ran his hands through his hair in frustration. "It's not what you think. Donny said she left a note, and all her clothes were gone from her apartment. She's left, Antonio."

"Why would she leave?" My body gave out, and I collapsed into the chair beside Mia. "Especially now."

"I don't know. Donny is on his way with the note she left behind. You know how she is, *fratello*. Catarina has never wanted this life." Massimo looked broken.

He was right, though. She tried to distance herself from the family business, but we pulled her back in all the time.

Mia gave me a halfhearted smile as she held her hand out for me to take. I laced my fingers with hers and let her pull me back down into the seat beside her.

"I can't deal with this, Mia. First Michael, now Catarina." I closed my eyes and inhaled, trying to steady my nerves.

"Catarina left on her own by the sound of it. Maybe her letter will explain her reasons."

Deep down I knew she was right, but I couldn't help feeling everything was changing—and not for the better.

As I scanned the people surrounding us, I could see the same worry on their faces. Madison was tucked in Massimo's lap, her head resting against his chest. She'd become someone important to me, and not just as a sister-in-law. Madison helped me accept myself and gave me hope that my family would accept me as well. And they had, just as she predicted.

"You never did say why you're dressed like that." Mia tilted her head at me and cocked an eyebrow.

"It's not important." I shrugged, not wanting to admit what I had done. Mia knew I had a protective side. The dead man I left in her house months ago was proof of that. "What about you? You said you needed to talk to me about something."

"Yes—" A commotion near the nurses' station cut my words off. Vincenzo burst through the doors, causing me to jump to my feet, as did the others.

"They're here. My son and daughter."

"Congratulations, *fratello*." Massimo pulled him into a hug. "How is Riley?"

"Worn out. The babies came fast. Apparently, she has been in labor all day. Mia," Vincenzo turned to her, "You got her here just in time. Thank you." He pulled me into an unexpected hug.

"Well," Antonio cupped his shoulder and squeezed. "What

name did you give my niece and nephew? You've been keeping a tight lid on it."

Vincenzo's smile lit up the room. "Robert Deminico Anastasi and Veronica Gia Anastasi."

Massimo's eyes widened when he heard the names Vincenzo and Riley had picked. Deminico was his middle name, which meant one thing.

"You named him after me?" His face was full of pride, a radiant glow illuminating his features. His eyes sparkled with a sheer happiness, the corners crinkling as a broad smile spread across his lips.

"Yes. We gave him your middle name. And names after her parents. Massimo, if it wasn't for you, I would have fallen into despair long before Riley came into my life."

Seeing my brother get emotional wasn't something I was accustomed to. He was the stoic brother—the one who held it together when the rest of us were falling apart. I tensed when I spotted Donny standing off to the side, watching us closely.

"Donny!" I called out, alerting Massimo to his presence.

"Where's Catarina?" Vincenzo scanned the waiting room, expecting to see her there with Donny.

"She's gone." Donny handed over a folded note to Massimo and sighed. Her disappearance was affecting him just as much.

"What?" Vincenzo watched as Massimo read over the words.

Massimo held the letter out as if the words were burning his hand. "It says she's tired of everything and was going somewhere no one would find her. She promises she isn't in any danger and will come home… eventually."

"This is bullshit." Vincenzo snatched the letter from his grasp and clenched it in his fist as he read it himself. "This makes no sense. She promises she'll be safe from Ivanov where she's going. Donny?" He turned to my brother's right-hand man. "Where is she?"

"I don't know." His voice cracked. "And I know you need me here, but…" He hesitated. "I need to go look for her."

I couldn't take my eyes off him. How had we all missed it? Donny was in love with Catarina, and her disappearance was killing him.

"You love her?" I asked, holding his gaze intently. My eyes locked onto his, searching for any flicker of emotion or hint of a response.

He nodded. "I do. Maybe I should have told you all sooner, but she can be stubborn. She refused to let me in, and I fear it was me who pushed her away."

Massimo cleared his throat behind Donny. "Get Drew. He can take your place temporarily."

"You sure?" Donny stared at my brother searching for permission.

"Find my sister, Donny, and bring her home."

Donny dipped his head in thanks and turned to Vin and me. "Congratulations, Vin."

We watched as he hurried from the waiting room and disappeared into the elevator. "He'll find her." Massimo shrugged his shoulders as we watched him disappear from the parking lot.

I quirked a brow at Massimo. "You didn't act surprised about his confession."

"I've known for a long time he was in love with her—probably longer than he's admitted it to himself. Catarina couldn't ask for a better man. But he's going to have one hell of a time corralling her." Massimo chuckled as he pulled Madison into his arms.

"I'm going back to Riley. Once they move us to a permanent room, you can come visit."

We congratulated Vincenzo again and watched as he headed through the double doors. My stomach growled, reminding me I hadn't eaten in a while.

"I think Mia and I are going to go grab some food."

"Us, too. We'll come back in a few hours. They deserve some time alone before we bombard their room with visitors."

Drew took Madison and Massimo home, leaving Freddy to cart us around. Mia slid into the seat and grasped my hand. "Can we stop by the drugstore on our way home?"

I got Freddy's attention. "Freddy, can you make a pitstop at the Walgreens?"

"Sure thing, Sir."

My brows furrowed in concern. "Everything okay?"

"Yes… and no." Mia pursed her lips as she held my gaze, her eyes uncertain and confused. "I need to pick up a test."

"A test?" I shook my head in confusion. "What kind of test?"

"The kind that will confirm my suspicions."

I couldn't take my eyes off her as she spoke. The slow realization of what she was implying shook me to the core. "Are you?" I placed my hand on her abdomen as I held my breath.

"Maybe. Yes…" She groaned. "I don't know."

Words escaped me, so I did the only thing I could to convey my elation. I threaded my hand through her hair and pulled her mouth to mine. When the kiss broke, she rested her head on mine and whispered the words.

"You're not mad?"

"Mad?" I leaned back to look at her. "Why would I be mad?"

"The timing isn't exactly the best, and what if I'm carrying…" Her eyes closed, trying to mask the pain she was feeling.

I knew what she was thinking. What if the baby was Michael's? But the truth was, I knew this was a possibility in the unorthodox relationship we wanted with Mia. Children were something he and I both wanted, and it didn't matter who fathered them as long as we were all together.

"It doesn't matter who the father is, Mia." I tugged her hand into mine and placed a kiss to her knuckles. "In fact, I hope it is his. At least we will still have a part of him."

"Don't say that." Her voice hitched, breaking slightly as she spoke. "You act as though he's dead already."

Inhaling through my nose, I blew out a breath before speaking the words I had held off saying. "You saw the pictures. We have to prepare ourselves that he might not be coming back to us." My voice hitched with the words slipping from my tongue. We hadn't heard anything about his whereabouts, and the likelihood Ivanov still had him alive grew smaller and smaller with each passing day.

"Let's not think about it right now." I kissed her hand before threading our fingers again. "For now, let's see if you're pregnant."

We held onto each other the rest of the way to the store. This was supposed to be a happy moment for us. Regardless of the short time we had been together, I had fallen in love with her. Michael had as well. I suspected she loved him, too. Freddy left us in the car to retrieve what we needed. Mia clutched the brown paper bag against her chest as we rode home in silence. The walk upstairs felt enormous. Much like Vincenzo and Riley, our beginning was filled with turmoil and loss. In the darkest hours, we had found, then lost love.

Mia disappeared into the bathroom and when she appeared again—she huffed in frustration as she plopped down on the bed beside me. "We have to wait five minutes."

"You want me to go grab you something to eat?" I asked, concern lacing my voice.

"No," she replied, shaking her head, "My nerves are too shot to worry about food right now."

When the five minutes passed, Mia sat motionless on the bed. "You want me to go look?"

She nodded as she wrung her hands in her lap. I headed into the adjoining bathroom and paused. The tiny white stick sat precariously on the edge of the porcelain counter. I closed my eyes and picked it up.

Was my life about to change? The weight of that question bore down on me, mingling with the fear and hope swirling in my chest. *Could I be a father despite my heartbreak?* The uncertainty gnawed at me, but beneath it was a flicker of excitement, a possibility of something beautiful amid the chaos.

Stiffening my back, I took a deep breath, my heart pounding. I opened my eyes and looked down. The anticipation was almost unbearable. Two brilliant blue lines stared back at me, clear and undeniable. My fingers wrapped around the stick, and I palmed it tightly, the reality sinking in.

As I stepped into the bedroom, Mia glanced up, her eyes wide with anxiety. But then, slowly, a grin spread across my face, a mixture of disbelief and joy.

"Pregnant," I whispered, my voice filled awe.

The word hung in the air, a promise of a new beginning, a ray of hope piercing through the darkness that had enveloped us.

TWO WEEKS PASSED, and I still hadn't fully accepted that I was having a baby. Even as I stood there, holding Vincenzo's daughter, I was in disbelief at where my life had taken me. The tiny, warm weight of the baby in my arms felt surreal, almost like a dream I might wake from at any moment.

"You look good holding a baby," Riley smiled, her eyes twinkling as she stared up at her daughter, wrapped snugly in a blanket in my arms. "So?"

I knew what she was asking, even without the words. Antonio cut his eyes to her, then over to me, and smirked, his expression one of quiet joy and anticipation.

"So." I blew out my breath, feeling the weight of the moment. "It looks like we'll have kids close in age."

"I knew it!" Riley shouted, her voice filled with excitement, causing Robert to startle.

"Knew what?" Vincenzo scooped him up from the cradle set up in the living room and tucked him into the crook of his arm. Robert immediately quieted in the safety of his father's arms, the sight of it warming my heart.

"She's pregnant," Antonio said, breaking his silence. Until then, he had been silently watching me with the baby, his eyes filled with a mixture of awe and love.

"Pregnant?" His mother asked, her body perking up from her perch in the chair against the wall. His parents and sisters had arrived a day ago from Italy, and their presence added to the sense of family and belonging that filled the room.

"Yep." Antonio wrapped his arm around my waist and pressed a kiss to my temple, his touch grounding me. "We confirmed it the day the twins were born, then saw a doctor yesterday."

Vincenzo's eyes grew large with the proclamation. "That's amazing, Brother. When are you due?" He turned his questioning to me, his face alight with curiosity and happiness.

"Christmas," I replied, feeling a flutter of anticipation at the thought.

"I have to ask." My father pushed his hands into his pockets and bowed his head, his voice tentative. "Do you know who fathered the baby?"

"Father," Vincenzo growled, a protective edge to his tone. "That is of little importance."

"No, you misunderstand. I know you were in a committed relationship, the three of you. Massimo explained it all to me. I was only curious if you knew?"

"We don't." Antonio held me tighter, his grip a comforting anchor. "But we did a paternity test to find out."

"Why?" Riley gasped. Her eyes were wide with disbelief. "It shouldn't matter."

"It doesn't change how I will feel about her or the baby," Antonio explained, his voice thick with emotion. "We just want to know if Michael is here with us. Since we haven't…" He swallowed down his grief, the raw pain of Michael's absence evident in his eyes.

We just need to know," I said, hugging Antonio tightly against me. "Nothing more."

"Have you heard anything regarding Michael?" Antonio's father asked, his voice filled with genuine concern.

Their father was trying to help us as much as he could with the situation. He had learned that Ivanov had fled the country and was likely in South America. Massimo reached out to their new friends in Chile, making them aware of the new development. The Silva Brothers had already dealt with Ivanov on a personal level and were ready to kill him. Apparently, Matias, the eldest brother, was engaged to Ivanov's daughter, Katya. Ivanov had tried to kill his own daughter at the same time he had kidnapped Antonio. It was the Silvas who found him, bringing him home to Vegas. Since that moment, the Anastasias and Silvas had formed an alliance… more than an alliance. Along with the Sureños, they had become friends. They were both seeking vengeance on Ivanov. One of them would finally get it—we just didn't know who.

"No, there is no sign of him anywhere," Antonio's father said, his voice heavy with regret. "If he's dead, Ivanov would have dumped him where we would have found him. Otherwise, his death would be meaningless. I'm still holding onto the hope he is alive."

"We both are," I whispered into the room, placing my hand on my abdomen.

"Everything will work out, my dear." Antonio's father patted me on the arm as he took his seat beside his wife.

I could see the love between them and envied it. I could only pray Antonio, and I would survive the trauma of losing Michael and forge a love like theirs. He wanted to believe Michael was alive with the news that nobody had been found, but we both knew that it was like wishing on a star.

Catarina had not been found yet. Wherever she'd run to, she had chosen wisely. Donny was still gone, refusing to give up on locating her. Even if he found her, did he really think she would come back home? I didn't, but I kept that opinion to myself.

For now, Antonio and I would hold on to our hope and focus on this life growing inside me. We stayed a little longer before kissing the babies and bidding farewell to the family. With the knowledge that Ivanov was no longer in Vegas, Antonio and I had moved out of Vincenzo's place. We'd all been staying there for protection, but now it was a moot point. Antonio and I made the decision to move into Michael's house, where we could feel close to him with him still missing. As we pulled down the long drive, my phone rang in my purse. I fished it out and sucked in a breath.

"It's the doctor's office." I glanced over at Antonio as I pressed the speaker button. "Hello?"

"Miss Hill?"

Antonio laced his fingers with mine giving me the strength to speak. "Yes, this is her."

"This is Dr. Kimbel's office. We are calling with the results of your paternity test."

Antonio parked the car and cut off the engine. His knuckles were white as he gripped the steering wheel with his free hand and waited.

"Ok. You're on speaker, please… tell us." She took a deep breath stealing herself for the answer we both wanted but didn't want to hear.

"The results show the sample you provided from Mr. Anastasi has been excluded as a having a paternity match. I'm sorry, Miss Hill. It appears he's not the father."

I mumbled something in response before disconnecting the call, a strange numbness settling over me like a heavy fog. It felt surreal to hear the words, as if they belonged to someone else's life. Antonio pressed his hand to my back, the warmth of his touch bringing me back to the present, grounding me in the here and now. His eyes, filled with unabashed tears, reflected every emotion I was feeling—shock, sorrow, and an odd sense of relief.

"Antonio," I whispered, my voice barely audible, words failing me as the weight of the moment bore down on us both.

He pressed his lips to my cheek, the gesture tender and full of unspoken understanding. "I know," he murmured, holding me tightly against him as if trying to shield us both from the pain.

My head was spinning with the revelation of the news. Antonio wasn't the father. Michael was. The realization hit me like a tidal wave, a mix of overwhelming emotions crashing over me—grief for Michael's absence, hope for the new life growing inside me, and a bittersweet joy at the connection to him.

"He's with us, baby. Michael is with us," I whispered into the car, my voice trembling with emotion.

Antonio's hand moved to the slight curve of my belly, his touch gentle and reverent. "He's with us," he repeated softly, his voice filled with a fragile hope. The acknowledgment was a fragile thread of comfort in a world that had been turned upside down. It was our tiny miracle in the midst of despair, a beacon of light guiding us through the darkness.

We stayed like that for a long moment, wrapped in each other's arms, letting the tears flow freely. The enormity of our situation loomed over us, but in that instant, we found solace in the life we had created together. The future was uncertain, but we held on to the hope that, somehow, we would find our way through it.

The car felt like a sanctuary, a small bubble of safety in a chaotic world. Antonio's breath was warm against my skin, his heartbeat a steady rhythm that echoed my own. Together, we faced the unknown, united by our love for each other and for Michael, who remained an integral part of our lives. The tears continued to fall, mingling with whispered promises and shared grief.

We cried for the new beginning, for the unknown future that lay in front of us…

But most of all, we cried for Michael.

CATARINA

MY HEART RACED like a thousand horses stampeding across a field as I shoved everything I could into my bag. The urgency of the moment pressed on me, the fear of being discovered making my hands tremble. I was finally alone and knew this was my only opportunity to leave without my brothers finding out. The bag weighed heavily against my shoulder as my feet padded down the stairs of my apartment building. Each step echoed with the finality of my decision. The daylight burned heavy against my face as I stepped outside onto the curb, scanning for my ride. Leaving without a trace meant abandoning my car and most of my belongings.

As I slipped into the back of the cab, I gave one last glance at the place that had been my home since moving out on my own. At eighteen, I thought getting my own place and going to college would create some distance from the lifestyle the Anastasi family—my family—led. After pushing myself to graduate college early, I had finally managed to secure a job as an emergency room nurse. If only I had known my new skills would suck me back into the mafia world, I would have studied to be a teacher instead.

Countless times, my brothers had needed my help to patch someone up off the books.

Countless times, I had been dragged into the family dealings whether I wanted it or not.

Countless times, I was reminded I was an Anastasi.

I was *done*.

Done with the bloodshed and done with the fear of being killed or taken—simply because I was the daughter of the most powerful mob boss in Sicily and the sister to the current Don of Las Vegas. After being nearly kidnapped, I had started to formulate my exit plan and had been working on it for months without their knowledge.

I hated to leave them like this, but it was the only way.

I deserved a chance at a normal life, and staying here in Vegas would prevent that. The thought of never seeing my siblings again or my niece and nephew, who were due any day now, caused my heart to clench. This was the part I dreaded—the not being there for their arrival. But this was it. My only chance at disappearing into the world. I was smart enough to leave Donny a note, telling him I had simply left. With Dmitri Ivanov's threat still looming over us, I didn't want them to think he'd finally nabbed me.

The cab pulled up to the bus station and let me out. I had my dark hair tucked under a baseball cap and sunglasses shielded my eyes. It wasn't really a disguise, but it made me feel invincible to onlookers. A week ago, I had withdrawn most of my savings and put it into a new account under the fake name

I would now go by. It had cost me a shit ton of money to secure, but I needed every layer of protection I could get if I was truly going to start over.

The fumes of the exhaust filtered through the interior of the monstrosity I was using as my escape. It was the last place my brothers would think to look. A mafia princess like me would never be caught on public transportation, which made it perfect for my getaway. I moved through the aisle and situated myself in the back-corner seat. My bag was stowed beneath the metal frame with the other passengers' things, making me blend in like any other traveler. I watched as the bus filled with more people before finally closing its doors.

An elderly woman smiled as she stopped in the walkway beside me. "Do you mind if I sit here?"

"Not at all." I waved to the empty seat and watched as she plopped down then buckled up.

She tilted her head as she spoke. "Why is a pretty little thing like you traveling on a bus alone?"

I blew out my breath and smiled. "A new start."

"We can all use one of those from time to time. I'm Elenore." She held out her frail hand for me to shake. "I guess we're going to be bus mates."

I slipped my palm into hers and smiled. "I'm Trina. It's a pleasure to meet you, Elenore."

We fell into a simple conversation about her life and my reason for moving. She was excited to learn I was going to be living in the town she was from—she even hinted at wanting to introduce me to her grandson.

"That's kind of you, but I…" I began, hesitating.

"Is there a man you're leaving behind?" Elenore asked, her eyes twinkling with curiosity.

"It's complicated," I replied, sighing deeply.

"Love always is, my dear," she said with a knowing smile. "Well, if you change your mind, let me know. I hope we can be friends once you're settled."

"I'd like that, Elenore," I said sincerely, feeling a sense of warmth and comfort from her presence.

"You're going to love our little town. And the hospital too. Everyone is so welcoming," she assured me, her voice filled with genuine enthusiasm.

I hoped she was right. When I stumbled across the job opening, I was elated. It was far enough away and completely opposite Vegas. I was sure it was the perfect place to start over. Getting the job was a bit trickier than I expected since I had to do it under my fictitious identity. Fortunately, my supervisor was willing to take a nice payment to lie for me and keep it a secret from my family.

I must have dozed off at some point during our ride because I woke up to Elenore shaking my shoulder.

"Wake up, sleepy girl. We're almost there."

I yawned and stretched as I took in the landscape out the window. Night had fallen, but the tiny town was lit up nicely. Everything about the view made my insides clench with possibilities. It was the first time in my life I was truly alone. I couldn't contain the smile that spilled across my face when the bus drove past the city limit sign. This was it. This was my new life.

Welcome to Lake District, Oregon. Population 7k.

What would you risk for the one who got away?
When the woman he loves becomes a pawn in a dangerous game, he'll stop at nothing to save her—even starting a war.

Can Catarina fight her way back to him, or will their love burn in the chaos?

Grab Deadly Intentions, Book Four of the Anastasi Family Syndicate next to find out!

bonus scene

VINCENZO

I SPUN the blade in my hand, watching as the metal glinted in the light seeping into the warehouse. I had sworn all those years ago that I wasn't this person anymore, but Dmitri had resurrected this side of me. And now, it was time for him to meet the monster.

I pressed the tip against Dmitri's chest, applying the smallest amount of pressure.

"Do you feel it?" I asked. Dmitri grunted something unintelligible.

"What? Did you say something?" I taunted, digging the sharp edge into his skin and slipping it between his ribs.

Leaning in closer, I pushed the blade deeper. "You deserve to die a thousand times," I hissed.

Dmitri cried out, barely holding on to consciousness. I grabbed his hand and, with slow, deliberate precision, began to remove his fingers, one by one. Each finger dropped to the ground with a sickening thud as it hit the cement.

"No more," Dmitri managed to plead, his voice barely a breath. The sound only enraged me further.

"Didn't Katya beg you for no more? What about Michael? Didn't he beg you to stop? Fuck you, Dmitri. No more talking." I forced his mouth open and removed his tongue.

The sound of retching behind me drew my attention to the door. One of Matias's men was getting sick. I gave him a warning look. "I told you this would happen."

The man nodded, wiping his face. I knew I must look like a monster, but this had been a long time coming.

"Do you remember when your goon stabbed me? When I find him, his death will be quick... unlike yours. But know this, Dmitri, he will die."

I was done toying with him. I shoved the knife into his throat and drew it out, watching as blood poured down onto the cement, coating the dirty floor in crimson. I stepped back as Dmitri's head rolled from his body onto the floor. I had severed the head from the snake.

Matias, standing off to the side with Cristian and Bastian, glanced at the pool of blood spreading across the floor. His gaze was hard, but his eyes betrayed something else—an emotion he wasn't used to showing. Rage, we all knew, but the weight of justice, long overdue, seemed to burden him.

Bastian clenched his jaw, his hands balled into tight fists, trying to hold in the fury still surging through him. Cristian, quieter than the rest of us, wiped his hands clean of the violence, but nothing would wash away the feel of Dmitri's blood on our hands.

I stood there, staring at Dmitri's decapitated head, my breath coming in uneven bursts. The adrenaline was wearing off, but the pain lingered, lodged deep in my chest. I thought about what Dmitri had done, how many lives he had destroyed. Catarina's broken, fragile face flashed before me, and I thought of Michael, who was still missing.

And Katya.

The image of Dmitri torturing his own daughter flickered in my mind, igniting a fresh wave of disgust and anger. How could a man, a father, do that to his own flesh and blood? It made me sick.

Without thinking, I clenched the blade in my hand, my knuckles white against the hilt. I had lost count of how many times I had plunged it into Dmitri's flesh, but it wasn't enough. It would never be enough. Nothing could make up for the torment he had caused.

"You should have suffered more," I whispered, my voice hoarse and barely audible.

Bastian was the first to move, placing a firm hand on my shoulder, grounding me. "He's gone, Vin. He's gone."

I took a deep breath, my body rigid as I tried to release the rage still simmering inside me. Slowly, I loosened my grip on the knife, letting it drop to the ground with a dull clatter. I wiped a hand across my face, smearing the blood. But it didn't matter. Nothing mattered except that Dmitri was finally dead. The monster that had haunted us for so long was gone.

Masimo, ever the cold and methodical one, finally broke the silence. His voice was low, like the final toll of a death knell. "It's done. We'll be home tomorrow. No, he didn't give up

Michael's location. I know, Bella. I love you, too." He shoved his phone into his pocket and sighed. "Call Riley, Vin. She'll ground you. And check on your babies. Burn the body. Let there be no trace left of him. No memory. No mercy."

I closed my eyes for a moment, exhaustion washing over me. The violence had been necessary, but it had taken something from me, something I wasn't sure I could ever get back. I flicked open my phone and dialed the one person who could anchor me.

"Vin?" Riley's voice brought me back to the present. Just hearing her eased the tension in my body, if only slightly.

"Yes. It's over, Tesoro. Dmitri is gone. He'll never threaten us again." The sound of a baby's cry drifted through the phone. "Is everything okay?"

She sighed, relief palpable. "Everything is perfect. Robert is always hungry, so he's protesting right now."

I laughed softly. "He's like his father. When he wants his mother, he gets impatient. How is Gia?"

"Sleeping. They miss you. I miss you."

"We're coming home soon. First, we need to make sure everything is okay here. One of Matias's men gave up the safe house. We don't know if the women are—" I paused, rubbing my head.

"Oh no. Vincenzo, go. Find out if they're okay. I'll be here when you come home."

"I love you, Riley. More than you'll ever know."

"Ditto, baby. Ditto."

Masimo nodded toward the door. "Let's go. We need to track down the safe house."

We moved in unison, like the well-oiled machine we had always been, but there was an unspoken weariness between us now. Dmitri was gone, but the scars he left behind would take much longer to fade.

I pocketed my phone and joined Masimo in the car. "How's Madison?"

"Eager to find Michael. She refuses to get married until we find an answer... one way or another."

"She loves Antonio," I said with a small smile.

"She does. They have a special bond. But I hate that she's had to postpone this so many times. And now, Catarina is gone. What the fuck was she thinking?"

As we climbed into the car, the conversation shifted, but the weight of what we had just done hung in the air like a specter. Catarina's disappearance, Michael's kidnapping—it was all still there, gnawing at us even as we focused on the task at hand.

"I don't know, Fratello. But if anyone will find her, Donny will."

"You're right. He's been in love with her for a long time. Maybe he'll be the reason she comes home."

I went quiet for a moment, thinking. I had wondered what had driven Catarina to run. For a long time, I thought it was the family lifestyle, but now, hearing Masimo's words, I wondered if it was something else. Something we hadn't seen.

"I hope you're right, Masimo. I hope he can bring her home."

"Why wouldn't he be able to bring her back?" Masimo asked, glancing over.

"Because we assume we know why she ran. But what if we were wrong? What if it had nothing to do with the family business?"

Massimo tilted his head, confused. "I don't understand."

"What if the reason she ran isn't a 'why'... but a 'who'?"

The possibility hung in the air, dark and unsettling, a thought none of us had considered. But now that it was there, it wouldn't go away.

Masimo's eyes widened in realization. He hadn't thought about that. Catarina might be running from the very person we sent after her. That only meant more trouble. He put the car in gear, pulled out of the lot, and was silent for a long moment before finally breaking the silence.

"Fuck."

Check out the Matais, Cristian and Bastian in the Silva Brothers Trilogy with book one: Blood Ties. Only at www.alphabookboyfriends.com

playlist

Dear God *(Ruben)*

Fire on Fire *(Sam Smith)*

To Die For *(Sam Smith)*

Him *(Sam Smith)*

I Don't Know What Love Is *(Lady Gaga, Bradley Cooper)*

Lie *(NF)*

Complicated *(Olivia O'Brien)*

hate you love you *(Olivia O'Brien)*

Love in the Dark *(Leroy Sanchez)*

Perfectly Wrong *(Shawn Mendes)*

Consequences *(Camila Cabello)*

Love Me or Leave Me *(Little Mix)*

Sorry *(Halsey)*

Hold On *(Chord Overstreet)*

Run To You *(Lea Michele)*

Out of Love *(Alessia Cara)*

As I am *(Justin Beiber with Khalid)*

At My Worst *(Pink)*

If Our Love is Wrong *(Calum Scott)*

Listen Here on Spotify

pulitano/anastasi family history

While the characters in this story are entirely fictional, their names are not. The majority of the character names came from my family tree. Of course, I took some liberties and altered how names were paired. Vincenzo Pulitano was my great-great-grandfather, and his history inspired the Anastasi Family Syndicate family names.

Vincenzo Mario Pulitano was born in 1882 in Bovalino, Reggio di Calabria, Calabria, Italy. He immigrated to Massachusetts, USA, around 1903. He met and married his wife, Celestina Anastasi, in Boston. They had five children, including a son who died shortly after birth. One of the five was my grandmother, Annette Pulitano.

After coming to the US, Vincenzo went by the Americanized version of his name, which is found in later American records as "Vincent." He was a barber and owned his shop until he lost his business during the Great Depression.

Two of Vincent's brothers, Michele and Carlo, also immigrated to Boston, where they later married._He likely had other siblings. Notes from a granddaughter also mention two brothers and a sister, unnamed. The occupations of the brothers in her notes are "priest" and "schoolmaster"; however, the two brothers found in the records for the City of Boston are both married.

Vincent died about Mar 1949 in Medfield and was buried at St. Michael's Cemetery in Boston, Massachusetts.

This information is readily available on my family Wiki Tree.

Check out more https://www.wikitree.com/wiki/Pulitano-5

about dori

"Love, Loyalty, and the Occasional Gunshot."

Dori Pulitano, a USA Today Bestselling Author, is the naughtier, much dirtier half of Author LC Taylor. Writing men in shades of grey, the bad girl Dori embraces her Italian side with heroic hitmen, decadent conflicted dons, and oh-so-f*ckable assassins trying to trade their devilish ways for salvation —and the perfect woman to tie to their bed.

And F**k following the rules... this author is most definitely trigger-happy.

Visit www.AuthorDoriPulitano.com to learn more.

facebook.com/AlphaBookBoyfriend

instagram.com/alphabookboyfriends

tiktok.com/@alphabookboyfriend

bookbub.com/authors/dori-pulitano